Flood Me With Fire

Maryann Chinelo Meniru

Flood Me With Fire

Copyright © 2020 by Maryann Chinelo Meniru

All rights reserved. This book or any portion thereof may not be reproduced or used in any manner whatsoever without the express written permission of the copyright holder except for the use of brief quotations in a book review.

This is a work of fiction. Names, characters, businesses, places, events, locales, and incidents are either the products of the author's imagination or used in a fictitious manner. Any resemblance to actual persons, living or dead, or actual events is purely coincidental.

Cover Artwork by Jude Chinedu Meniru

Cover Design by Maryann Chinelo Meniru

Editing by Dr. Godwin I. Meniru

ISBN 9798619098877

Part 1

Madame Inger sauntered down the hallway, her ankles rolling around in her oversized heels. They were borrowed from someone else's closet, along with her silver circlet, but no one had to know. Her stiff and starched proper suit was stretched to fit, but she carried herself with an envious confidence.

She entered the dining room at exactly eight o'clock. The team of servants was pitifully small, probably because of the lack of royals living in the palace and the eerily quiet halls. No one wanted to set foot in a palace that had burned to the ground eight years ago; one that was supposedly filled with ghosts.

Inger was the only permanent resident. It did not bother her that one of the ghosts was her own sister.

"Where's Miscellanea Daniels?" she grumbled, tucking a napkin into her collar so nothing ruined her pant suit. "I'm not eating until she gets here."

Cleo, one of the servants standing closest to the table was prompted to offer her tea. Inger scowled.

"I just said I'm not eating until Miss Daniels gets here. Why must I doubly explain everything to you servants?"

Cleo backed away. "Now Madame—"

The wide French doors to the dining room opened, and a pale, pig-nosed woman stood there, breathless from running. It was the infamous Miss Daniels.

"Sorry, I think the cold froze my fuel tank, then the roads were a nightmare. It took a millennium to even leave my driveway."

"No excuses. Come sit. My food is getting cold since I was kind enough to wait for you." Inger turned up her short nose and snorted. She then dropped down into a wooden chair draped with embroidered red cloth. Miss Daniels watched from the entryway.

The second Inger sat, servants rushed forward, lifting metal covers off the serving trays. Steam rose to the high-strung chandelier, curling and willowing back down with a savory aroma. Miss Daniels was quick to sit down when she saw what was being served; fresh cheese, created in flawless wheels from Pigladen, egg whites fried with tomatoes, onions, and peppers on top of thick slices of wheat-rolled bread topped with slices of fresh avocado. Bacon in generous servings, sausage links and towers of some sort of tofu roll. Pastries, light and flaking, and filled with fruit jam. Miss Daniels grunted in delight when servants started filling her plate while Cleo poured her a glass of fresh-squeezed orange juice.

She was digging into her plate for a few minutes, and Inger let her until the silence grew annoying. She cleared her throat, promptly signaling her guest to pay attention. Miss Daniels straightened, folding her hands until her knuckles turned white.

"Servants, you may leave," Inger ordered. "We are having a private meeting."

The room was quickly and eagerly deserted. Miss Daniels licked her lips anxiously, trying to look presentable again. It did not work, since she had never been a particularly presentable individual.

"Our plan has been compromised," Inger said through her teeth. "I may not be queen next year."

"Why, Inger? The public seems satisfied with the idea now. Besides, there's no one to take your place." Miss Daniels lowered her voice. "We went through some well-planned schemes eight years ago."

"No."

Miss Daniels gasped, her eyes widening. The decadent meal was as good as forgotten.

"Arabella swears she saw her." Inger did not have to specify who *she* was.

"Everyone sees her. It's what happens when someone dies. Ever since your scientist age-processed her picture, everyone is trying to find a lookalike to fit the conspiracy. That's all it is, a conspiracy theory to get everyone's minds racing for another few months until they forget again."

"She should be dead." Inger frowned. "If someone finds her, and puts her on the throne…"

"She's dead Inger. Don't doubt yourself."

"We were never completely sure."

"She's dead," Miss Daniels said firmly.

"I think she's alive. It's time to put the team to work again." Inger slammed her fist on the table, disturbing every delightfully-filling dish. "Don't tell me to stop looking again. I won't stop searching until this idea, this belief, is dead. I want the lost daughter of Princess Cyrana Lagarde to be found once and for all."

***

Luck

It was a terribly cold day in Cyan. Snow fell lazily from the sky, turning into brown slush on the roads. Even though Maude had a fire going in her fireplace, I was still numb and icy. I slid closer to her rocking chair, pulling the skirt of my gown out from under me and folding it over my cold arms. Maude ignored me for the most part, but she did shift a corner of her blanket over the edge of the chair so I could rest my head on it. She'd be nice to me until I started bugging her again.

We were sisters, but we looked nothing alike. Maude was seventeen, three years older than me, with long straight brown hair and eyes. She was petite and a little stockier than me, with a tanner, rounder face. I had blonde curls that stopped at my shoulders, with big, green eyes. People said my green eyes reminded them of lucky clovers, which was why my nickname, Luck, caught on so quickly, but Mama said there were other reasons. I was nearly Maude's height, but trimmer. I was also way ahead of my grade level, which was why I was going to Etiquette Boarding School a whole two years ahead of everyone else. At least, I would know once the letter came in.

In short, there was nothing I couldn't handle.

"Maude," I whined indignantly. "Tell me why Mama and Papa are sleeping in separate rooms again."

"You're too young, Lucienne," Maude calmly replied, not even looking up from her homework from Principles. That was the posh school she went to most days, on the other side of Cyan City. "I don't want you being exposed to this kind of drama. Mama and Papa are fine."

"You say that like I'm too dull to know better." I sat up on my knees, propping my elbows up on the arm of her chair. "Don't you think it's peculiar?"

"Mama snores. Maybe Papa wanted a restful night."

"Don't lie to me."

"Lady Lucienne Legrand," Maude snapped, at her wit's end. "Please leave my room, I'm trying to study."

I frowned, temporarily defeated.

"Fine, Maude. I just have one more question."

She rolled her eyes. "This better not be about those magazines you were reading yesterday after dinner."

"They had scholarly articles in them."

"According to who?" Maude turned the page in her notebook dramatically, signaling that I should really stop bothering her.

I tapped my chin, too curious for my own good. "You were older than me when the Burning happened."

"What are you getting at, Luck? You're always talking about these crazy stories and legends."

"People are talking about the rumors again, the ones about the princess, saying she's still alive. You know, Inger, won't be our leader if the princess is found alive."

"Luck." Maude glared at me. "You really shouldn't say things like that."

"This isn't a dictatorship," I said. "I can say whatever I want. No one's listening."

Maude flipped the page again. I was pretty sure she had stopped reading several minutes ago. "The world isn't what it used to be. Trust me."

"You're only three years older than me. How much could I have missed?"

"A lot." Maude held the notebook up higher, obscuring her face. "You really shouldn't believe everything you see on those gossip pages."

"I'm not a supporter of Inger, if you ask me. The whole country probably agrees." I twisted a corner of the blanket around my finger, watching it redden against the yellow fabric. "Why is it that no one cares what Inger does?"

"Say that a little louder and we'll really be in trouble."

"Come on, Maude. You always say I don't know anything, but you won't even answer me." I stood up and gathered my things. If she was not willing to talk then I would just have to figure out on my own.

I guessed that Maude did not have time to listen to me ramble on and on about what I had read up online or seen on the television. We used to spend hours together, sitting up at night, talking about anything and being equally annoying. College had taken that side of Maude away from me, and it did not seem like she cared half as much as I did.

Maude would be leaving for another school trip soon, and I would have no one's nerves to get on, until she came back. That would be after I'd started at Etiquette, and then when would we have time to see each other?

I took my magazines next door to my room and curled up on the floor, flipping through the pages alone. Suddenly the article I was going to show her did not seem so interesting anymore.

Oh well. I would give her thirty minutes, and then go back over again.

I rolled over onto my stomach, distracted by one of the printed images taking up two whole pages. They had recently painted the exterior of Etiquette again, making it even more gorgeous than before, ready for the new class starting soon. I should have been beside myself with excitement, but in the moment, I was apprehensive.

Leaving home was part of everyone's life. It had to happen at some point. At least I would still be in the city, and my family would be easy to reach.

If they were still together.

I could not shake the feeling that everything was going to change, and the world I left behind when I went to Etiquette would disappear. I knew Maude had her trip, but with everything else potentially happening at home, what was I to expect?

For half a second, I wondered if I should have turned down my admission and stayed homeschooled. *No. That's ridiculous. Who would pass up this kind of opportunity?*

I sat up, closing the magazine and smoothing the seam over my leg. There was no need to start worrying now. I would get myself all worked up, and then where would I be? Out of school having missed out on something so many other people could only dream of happening in their lives.

I checked the clock on the wall, deciding how to spend the next half hour.

Maude had gotten off the hook for now, but I was going back once the time was up. I only had so many more days to spend with my best friend before both of us went our separate ways.

***

Pizzette

Kids ran away from home all the time. They always had good reasons. At least, I thought so.

Would mine even qualify if I decided to go for it?

No, Pizzette. Everyone would point at you and shake their heads because you're being ridiculous.

I sat on my plush bed, gazing around my purple-painted room. Pictures hung on the walls, of me with my old friends, me in front of the Gallery Theater while Mom fretted behind the camera. Pictures of me going back to school, eight years ago to just a few months. Pictures of every event I did not want to forget after my eighth birthday started somewhere in a haze of jumbled memory. All of them tacked into the thick wood walls with now rusting nails from the humidity. I would need to bring them with me. I would not forget my past again.

I smelled the familiar scent of lavender wafting up from my romper, a gift I recently received for my sixteenth birthday. My hair had also been trimmed for initiation into the new society we would be entering, since flyaway dull cedar hair down to one's waist was apparently too… What was the word Mother had used? Immature? A sign of low class? After I picked out a nice ensemble for a present, she pulled me into one of Bark's few shopping malls; we left with bags upon bags of dresses and material for gowns. And me, with my hair several inches shorter and my bangs evened out and pressed flat against my forehead. Mom even bought a bracelet, ring, and circlet set made of sterling silver and steel-cut diamonds that would help me *make friends*. At least she had not asked me to change out the necklace I always wore around my neck.

My father's diamond. That was all he left behind. A heart cut out of diamond with silver chains encasing it on a string of connected loops and a chest full of twenty million cizotes in diamonds that Mom had taken a portion of and changed to Bark notes. I was eight, or close to it, when he died. Mom never liked to talk about him and our life before then.

My fingers tightened around the heavy rock. "Sorry," I said to the diamond, as if there was someone at its core. "Moving is just making me nervous."

Why was Mom making us move now? And back to the city where my father died?

It was not like Bark was a bad country to live in. We were residents of the Angelos Province. I had my Angelos citizenship card. Not a Cyan one. I could not even speak Cyan French.

I spoke Bark's language and English fluently. I tried telling this to Mom. She just said I would learn at Etiquette Boarding School.

That was our main reason for leaving. I would be getting a better education and graduate with the title of Lady, appointed by Madame

Inger herself. Etiquette was the smaller castle next to the palace, and supposedly, I was going to feel like *real royalty*.

Mom was going to force me to go to this new school, and all for a title? We were already wealthy, and titles had never bothered me. I knew she had other reasons that she would normally share, but this time, even as her daughter, I was not given clearance.

If I left, I would be caught. No one could escape the system. It was too constricting. As far as Pigladen they had your face mapped out and saved in the system so even if you managed to get away, someone would find you in the future.

I stayed locked in my room all day, packing every piece of my life into a small brown box. It was already filled, so whenever I sat on it trying to zip it shut, clothes fell out and I grew more annoyed.

It was ridiculous. Mom did not want us taking our old lives into Cyan, as if we would infect the city. The impression I had gotten thus far was not leading me to think we would be welcomed with open arms. It seemed like we were trying to sneak in under everyone's noses.

We were leaving tomorrow, riding the train like common people and arriving sometime the next day. The only thing I could not understand was why I was going to an elite private school instead of remaining fully undercover. It was like Mom could not make up her mind. The two of us comprising a lousy family were wealthy enough, but we did not belong there.

Growing up in Bark did not make me regal or posh, it made me unkempt and disorderly, according to her assessment. My grades were good enough, but I would not shine next to anyone in Cyan.

My French was abysmal. I was not pale and elegant. I would trip over my skirt and break my heels.

Average people like me stayed where they were meant to be, in between the elites and the failures.

***

It was snowing.

Snow and cold rain did not mix. The child found herself slipping and sliding down the street. The skirts of her upper-class frock nearly brushed the mud, but she held it up with her gloved hands as she hurried along.

Marmi was missing. She had to file a report.

She did not really know how. She was only eight years old and heard Marmi talking about it as she stirred the stew for dinner a few months ago. *Now, if someone goes missing, Pet, you go to the police and file a report. That way, their pictures and information are sent to all the surrounding provinces. Now why don't you finish your reading for tonight?*

She would go hungry if Marmi did not come home. The child could barely slice a loaf of bread as it was. Marmi never bothered her with chores, but she took it upon herself to try to learn anyway. Marmi always said it did not bother her, that it was better to stay indoors and carefree. The child could never understand why.

She came to the police station's door, mud on her nice white shoes.

Oops. That would send Marmi over the edge.

She opened the door, removed her very grown-up looking hat, and hung it on a peg by the door like adults did.

Her presence caught the attention of a few policemen standing by the front desk of the nice and clean office. One of them put down the cigarette he was smoking while another simply grinned, trying hard not to laugh at the spectacle. Another's face became curious.

The child's black curls swayed as she confidently walked towards the third. "I'd like to file a missing person's report."

The man looked down his nose at her. "Who are you? Who are you looking for?"

"My name is Petrakova Selle. My guardian, Marmi… Sorry, Marlene Selle is missing."

His face instantly became sympathetic. "You've been alone? For how many days?" The man flicked his hand, indicating someone should bring a clipboard and note paper to him.

"Two days. She said she would be back. I only waited because I thought she would keep her word."

"What is your name again?"

"Petrakova Selle. I need help." She paused, her face falling as she tried to think of anything else to say that would be useful. "I just turned eight, and she's the only family I have."

"Come to the waiting room and let me get your picture." The man was looking quite excited now. "Wait for a spell."

Petrakova followed obediently, oblivious. She had no other options. *Don't worry, Marmi. Me and this nice man are going to find you safe and sound.*

"Give me five minutes, and I'll be right back."

***

Luck

I passed Mama on my way to the kitchen where Polly was sorting the mail. Mama frowned, saying, "Please stop running. That's one of your dresses for Etiquette, and it needs to last the semester."

"They've sent out the schedules. I don't want to miss anything. I need to find out if they want to interview me."

"That is no reason to run, especially in your attire."

I ignored her and entered the kitchen. Normally, I would stop and admire the high domed ceiling with skylights fit into the sides. Look at the grey sky through the panes, the bare branches of the trees that surrounded our compound sway in the wind. Polly and Tor were always cooking something wonderful, and if they were feeling generous, they would let me have an extra snack outside my schedule.

Today, I nearly knocked Polly over as I descended on the pile of letters. There were the usual bills and taxes that were a joke since ours were always paid in advance. Letters from the different charities we funded. Letters from other noble families inviting us to parties and notes from families thanking us for hosting them. And there were always letters from nobodies trying to become friends with us Legrands.

I found the one from Etiquette, silver paper with gold trim and *Lady Lucienne Legrand* stamped across the front.

Tor was busy at the stovetop, his back towards me. "Lady, did you want something to eat?"

I quickly tore open the envelope, skimming the letter until I found what I had been looking for.

Mama walked into the kitchen. "Tor, you know she isn't supposed to eat so many snacks between meals."

I screamed and threw my arms around her, cutting off her scolding. "Winter Term starts in a week," I exclaimed, jumping up and down. "We have to go to the store again. I need so much."

"Well…" Mama's face brightened, looking a little cheerier after this morning's debacle. "I'm proud of you, Luck. I know you worked very hard at home to skip the last levels of school."

Polly was collecting the letters I had knocked over. She gave me a small smile, and then looked at Mama, her face suddenly grave. *"C'est encore cette femme."*

I looked at them skeptically. French was not one of my strong subjects.

"What did you say, Mama?"

"Tear it up. I'll talk to Louis when he returns." Mama let go of me, her eyes darkening. "Luck go study. Tor don't bring her anything. She needs to focus on her reading now."

"Wait." I pouted, crossing my arms. "Can't I relax a little more?"

"Now, Lucienne." I knew when she used that tone of voice, I had to listen. But still, a few extra hours of studying were annoying. I made it into the greatest school in the country. Was that worth nothing?

"Don't forget the interview," I muttered, turning on my heel.

"It's too early. We just received the acceptance letter."

"I want to be the first higher education applicant to be interviewed, okay?" I crossed my arms and frowned, which I knew was immature, but surprisingly, she agreed.

"Fine, but it's going to be a waste of time."

***

Inger slammed her fist on the table, disturbing a cup of pencils she never wrote with. *Why, of all days, must today be the day my life is ruined again?*

"That Marlene Selle was lying," she sputtered, crushing her glass in her hands. Icy liquid dripped all over her pale fingers and spilled onto the maroon rug on the ground. "Someone from the sheriff's office called the palace. A girl called Petrakova came in looking for her. Compare that to the narrative we got from Marlene; she lived alone and never raised a child. She was never involved in any of this."

"Now, Inger," Miss Daniels started, her eyes drawn to the red liquid running down the table. "Should I call someone to clean that? Don't lose your mind now. We've seen this happen before."

"Are you daft? We have a potential lead in this cold case, more promising than the first, and a rat in our holding. I was hoping my suspicions were wrong, and she never had anything to do with this. I've had enough of her already."

"You're climbing out on a limb and stressing yourself out." Miss Daniels hovered between her chair and standing, further aggravating

Inger with her indecisiveness. "I thought you cut ties with Marlene years ago."

"I had to keep tabs on her," Inger sighed heavily, hanging her head. "I know that much, but we need to be sure before we let this one go. Selle has been hiding this girl for eight years, which points strongly to her identity being what we fear it is. There are hair, blood and other samples in the labs below us that were ordered a millennium ago. We're going to test this one, even if we're wrong."

There was no stopping her once she was this set on a target. Miss Daniels finally gave in, dropping her own napkin on the table and rising. "Well, we shouldn't stall. I'll get the driver."

***

Petrakova woke to what sounded like thunder.

Her jaw had gone slack and her wrists were tied to the wooden chair the guards had given her to sit on. The door of the small, windowless room was shut tight. She heard voices on the other side of the door, what sounded like scared French spoken by a foreigner who put in immense effort.

"Hello?" Petrakova whispered, sitting forward. *Did they find Marmi? Is that why it's so chaotic?*

No response came. Her throat was getting dry. "Is anyone there? Why am I tied up?" *And when did I fall asleep?*

It was easy to slip her hands out of the ropes. Obviously, the person who tied her up did not expect much from someone so small.

These people aren't good. They don't want to help me find Marmi.

She had to get out of there.

Petrakova raced over to the door, terrified when the handle would not budge.

"Help me." Petrakova beat her fists against the door, gasping. Someone was yelling on the other side. She stopped screaming for a spell and listened to their voices.

Heart racing, Petrakova kicked at the stiff wood. "Don't lock me up. I'm only eight."

Someone answered her cries by slamming something against the door.

Petrakova sniffled, backing away. She was trapped.

"Okay, I'll sit down." She pulled her knees up to her chin, and waited on the chair, never taking her eyes off the door.

***

Luck

I sat in the polished and modern waiting room in Etiquette's admission office with my hands folded in my lap, and my new green lace gown flowing to the floor like a curtain.

"Lucienne, we came too early. I told you no one would be here to take your meeting if we arrived as soon as our letter did," Mama muttered, taking a sip of tea from the bounty a servant had set up for us.

"I was too excited Mama. I can't believe I'm actually inside Etiquette right now." I tried to push the nerves out of my voice, but my knee was bouncing up and down, and I could not look at the teapot and little cakes without feeling sick. If I messed this up, I would not be considered for a Lady Royal title. The leading monarch, Inger Kaleon in our case, assigned that title, and since I was already a lady, I could not graduate with anything less. Lady Royals were important; they had special duties and responsibilities to serve the crown, so I could not afford to portray myself as an immature and underage candidate.

"Lucienne, sit still. They could be watching you right now." Mama's voice was stern, her composure so tight her back did not touch her chair.

A servant came to refill her cup. "Madame Inger has left the palace. Your interview will be rescheduled."

I tried not to show my dismay. "Okay. I can wait." I reached for a dainty cup, wondering if anyone had ever drunk out of it before.

I burned my tongue.

"Obviously you are not ready for this commitment and should be delighted by a few hours of independent study," Mama scolded, grabbing my hand. "We're going home and coming back another day."

"Should I call a cab?" The servant was still standing there, her oblong face confused.

"Why can't Inger just be on time?" I asked, tugging on Mama's arm.

"It's Madame Inger Kaleon to you, and I don't know." Mama paused, handing the servant a couple cizotes to get the cab. "And you shouldn't care."

***

Inger's golden coach sailed through the streets. Miss Daniels was beside her, cringing every time they ran an intersection without stopping. The driver kept turning around and yelling at Inger for instructions, and she returned them out of order and with more anger each time he got them wrong.

"They have her locked in a room and unconscious," Inger whispered in French so the driver would not understand. "We are to simply retrieve and test the girl…What are you looking at driver? You just missed the turn."

"You told me something different five seconds ago," the driver muttered under his breath, putting the car in reverse and barreling into the wrong lane.

Inger switched back to French, which she dreaded speaking, the language still fluent after having lain dormant since her youth. "You and your husband are very good at cleaning up after us. I'll probably have Norm do the messy part."

"Yes ma'am." Miss Daniels turned to look out the window, a smirk lighting her face.

"Driver, this is the place," Inger said after a few more minutes of wandering. The coach stopped in front of the police office, the commotion within shrouded by its unassuming front lawn. "Wait here. This should only take a moment," she said to driver, and stepped out of the car with Miss Daniels.

***

Gigi Govette had been transferred to Cyan's detective department from Towering Heights less than a month ago. French had to be learned quickly, and her thick accent made her conversations with any of the snobby aristocrats here brief.

The office was chaotic. Officers swarmed the front of the building, and one stood next to the room where the child was confined. Gigi bent her head low, trying to focus on the papers on her desk. This was one of those cold cases she had hoped she would never have to reopen.

The child screamed again, and Gigi's shoulders stiffened. She looked up at the nearest officer, and in a disapproving voice asked, "Why does Inger want her so badly? Without even seeing her face?"

"You know why. Now be quiet and do your work," she snapped.

Gigi's fist tightened. *Jerk.*

The officer's collective attention turned to Madame Inger's golden coach visible through the front door's window. "Get ready to welcome her in."

They filed out the door, their backs to Gigi.

Gigi got up and tiptoed to the door. She was the youngest girl in this department, and everyone assumed she was just as quiet and boring as her work, so they had left the key easily within her reach. *I'm not a mouse, you idiots.*

She unlocked the door with shaking hands. The girl was awake, mumbling apologies in two languages.

"Get out of here. I'll open the back door for you." Gigi grabbed her hand and yanked her out of the room when she did not move fast enough, her long black hair whipping her in the face. She opened the door leading to the back lot, pushing her over the threshold. "Stay away from the police, please. They aren't going to help you if…Never mind."

"Thank you," Petrakova whispered, and then took off.

Gigi watched her go, and wondered, with a knotted stomach, how she was going to get out of this mess.

***

Inger was flattered by the array of respectful officers lining the cobblestone path for her. Their guns were held low, and their backs were impossibly straight.

Inger nodded perfunctorily to them; they bowed in unison.

"Where is the girl?" Inger asked Miss Daniels, still admiring their defenses.

"She's inside, Inger. Come in." Inger followed her inside the sheriff's office, the guards converging around her.

Gigi was sitting at her desk sorting letters. The door to the holding room hung ajar.

"She's gone," Gigi said casually without looking up at them. "I went to the bathroom and she wasn't there when I came back."

Inger's face darkened. "My time has been wasted then. Do not let this girl think she is so smart." Inger elbowed one of the guards, her admiration for them gone. "*Go.*"

"And do what? You can't accuse me of anything."

"I don't need to justify my decisions to you. Someone, arrest her."

Gigi swallowed hard before willingly stepping away from her desk to be handcuffed by one of her colleagues.

Inger's eyes swept the room, landing on a child-sized lacy hat. "Is this the child's?"

"Yes," the nearest officer confirmed. "She was wearing it when she came in, dressed up like an adult."

Inger pulled it off the peg and plucked several hairs from the inside. Inger held out her hand with her palm facing up, and Miss Daniels placed a glass tube on it. Inger smoothly tucked the hair strands into the tube.

"Thank you all. We'll be leaving now. My scientist will test this."

***

Pizzette

Mom and I arrived at the train station in the early hours of the morning. It was cold, and my stylish but thin cloak was doing a poor job of keeping me warm.

I sat amongst our boxes while Mom bought our tickets. The station was humming with life and noise. The other travelers seemed more excited about reaching their destinations than me.

I hummed an old lullaby while waiting, closing my eyes and trying to remember who had taught the song to me. It certainly was not Mom.

Tonight, I'll sing you a song,
Lift your smile.
I'll speak of a feather-light hand
Against your checkered cheek.
When you wake, little diamond,
You'll still be in a dream.

I had always smiled at the simplicity of the verse. That love could be so quickly found in a dream and that it could be kept forever.

"Pizzette. Our train is over here."

My eyes snapped open, the moment of peace in my dream world gone.

We were leaving. What was I doing still reminiscing about the past I did not even know?

Mom called someone to help us carry our boxes to the luggage car. I took one final look at Bark before stepping on board the train. I did not look back as the train left the station.

Mom and I sat in one of the elegant first-class coach compartments, the lavish space including two enormous portable television sets suspended from the ceiling. One was showing classic movies and the other was playing Cyan love songs.

Neither really interested me. I just sat there staring at my folded hands in my lap and let the noise fade together.

At some point, I fell asleep. When I woke up, two hours had passed, according to the clock in the bottom corner of one of the television screens. My attention was drawn to the live video broadcast. An arrogant-looking woman wearing clothes a size too large was on the screen. She was speaking in English, and even though she smiled, I was still bothered by the rest of her relatively inexpressive face.

"Hello, my people."

I wanted to snort. This woman was no leader. There was nothing commanding about her presence.

"I am Madame Inger, sister of the late Princess Cyrana."

My jaw dropped.

"And I am speaking today to tell my country about the heir to the throne." She paused, smiling like a cat. "I was voted to lead by my team of advisors. My coronation is quickly approaching. This country will soon no longer be without a solid leader."

That woman was about to be queen? I looked around at the disinterested people around me. I wanted to know more about where I was going, so hopefully they would not mind me changing the channel on one of the other televisions.

"Show me anything on Cyan's history," I whispered to the other television. The screen zapped black. The television hummed for a second, and then it displayed the logo for the information article.

I started to follow the words as they zipped by. The eighth anniversary of the Burning had already passed, an event I learned ended in a harrowing blaze that destroyed the palace and killed somewhere between one hundred and two hundred people, including the whole royal family. One of them was Princess Cyrana Lagarde, the wife of the also dead Prince Indio Hayes Lagarde. She had not been born royal.

"As we have passed over the eighth anniversary of this tragedy, new rumors and information have led to calls for a new investigation into the Burning. The previous conclusions reached by chief investigators ruled out arson and pre-meditated murder. The extent of the blaze, however quickly it seemed to spread before being detected, had been ruled as a mechanical failure of the palace's old electrical systems. No further evidence was ever presented to challenge this idea, until…"

Inger was all Cyan had left? She had been one of the few survivors of the Burning, a member of the commoner Kaleon family, and they had just taken her in because she was Cyrana's sister?

Looking at those pictures of the palace on fire was making my head spin. "Go back to the other channel. I'm done reading," I ordered. The television must have been an older model, because it got stuck on that image, the hum growing louder and louder until an attendant came down the aisle and tried to shut it off. It kept making noise.

"Pizzette, don't make a scene." Mom, who had been half asleep, suddenly turned my face away from the display. "Why were you watching that?"

"Mom, I don't want to go to Cyan anymore."

"Why? This is where you belong."

"That doesn't matter. I don't want to go anymore."

Mom sighed loudly, shaking her head. "We are not talking about this now. Not here."

"Isn't Etiquette right next to the new palace? I can't stay right next to a graveyard." The television stopped right before my last sentence. A couple people in the rows around us turned around and stared.

"Pizzette Marie-Rose Colfer."

"*Yes Mom?*"

"That is enough. We will talk about this in the future."

***

The train shot out a plume of smoke right before docking at the station in Cyan, which was tucked into the background like a bad stamp. With wobbling legs, I stood and followed the line of passengers exiting the train before it continued to its next stop.

I stepped off the platform onto smooth and unusually white cement. I smelled salty air. It was impossibly cold, and I wished I had worn a different cloak altogether.

Mom and I had to call a cab to carry us and our boxes to our home. All around us were Cyan's elegant, pale, and well-dressed citizens. I saw a girl my age walking hand in hand with an older boy, clearly flaunting her engagement ring for anyone who cared to look.

The cab arrived, spraying our feet from a nearby puddle. I was prepared to suffer through an awkward French exchange with a stranger, but to my surprise, they spoke English.

"Just get in. I'm freezing."

"Oh my God, you speak English! I was so worried I'd—"

"Did you hear me? Get in."

Right. I tried to hide my embarrassment as I scrambled into the cab with Mom, keeping my mouth shut.

We sailed down the white streets, the boxes bouncing around in the back. Rain splashed against the windows, disturbing my view of the pretty but fading city. It was as gray and dull as the sky, every tall building melding into the next. Even the signs and billboards seemed tinged with sadness. It looked like ash had settled here a long time ago, and no one had bothered to clean it up.

Our home was a respectable property on the outskirts of the city in a neighborhood called Tumbleweed Gardens. Up every long and winding driveway was a mansion shrouded in trees, with expansive yards and fountains. Dozens of cars lined the streets, as if there was a party at every destination.

"You know..." The driver peeked at us, or me, since I was the only one ogling. "You look like you've never seen a tree before. Did the Environment Restoration Act never get to your territory?"

"No, it's just that...this place is so wealthy, but they don't drive hover cars," I lied, my face burning. *At least try and act like you belong, and maybe you might fool the cab driver who picked you up from the train station.*

"The tech was so bothersome the Lagarde family never considered them. Cars can go more places anyway. They don't need all that hovering magnetic tech in the ground first." He stopped in front of a sloping hill, the gates the only indicator that there might be a house below. "Anyway, this is your stop. Danish Mansion. I don't feel like driving down the hill, so you can walk from here."

He left us with our stack of boxes and drove off. Mom wasted no time before entering the password in the lock system and opening the gate. We pushed the boxes down the hill, stopping when the house came into view.

It was older than some of the others in Tumbleweed Gardens, almost hidden by a thick crop of trees that must drop a horde of leaves in Autumn. It also looked like it had been vacant for a while.

The whole journey leading up to this point had not been enough to scare me, but now I was truly nervous.

***

We literally stood outside our mansion for ten minutes, gawking as rain dribbled down our arms.

Finally, I flipped my wet hair over my shoulder and grabbed my bags. They rolled suavely in the mud as I made my way to the door. I pressed my palm against the scanner, hoping it had already been programmed to recognize new visitors, or else we would have some problems.

"New Occupant; Pizzette Colfer." The rectangular box hummed, a light pink ray passing under my hand. "Name registered in databases. Permission granted by previous homeowner; Richard Nolatore."

"Mom hurry up and scan yours so we can go inside. I'm freezing."

Mom's face was a little paler as she laid her hand against the device. The scanner recited a similar greeting, and then the doors unlocked and let us inside.

I found a light switch against the wall and flicked it upward. The room that welcomed us was large, with a sweeping staircase to one side and a dusty chandelier above us. It was also completely devoid of furniture.

"They emptied the house," Mom said with a frown. "They weren't supposed to. I was told we'd have furniture. I bet the beds are gone too."

I laughed, shrugging my shoulders. "We should just go back. No one will have bought our house in Bark yet." I received a curt glare and closed my mouth.

Five minutes later, we were already tired of looking at an empty house with broken light fixtures and dusty windows and decided to pick out bedrooms upstairs. Mine was large like every room in this house and gaudy pink and white, with flouncy curtains pulled tightly away from a window that was probably not ever going to open again. The floors were splintery acacia wood, covered by a thin layer of dust.

I picked the cleanest corner and laid out a few towels and my crocheted blanket as a substitute bed. At this point, I was a little less annoyed about the whole Etiquette thing. At least I would have a dorm with furniture.

The bathroom off to the side was a little cleaner. The skylight above was entirely blacked out by fallen leaves, so I turned on a few faux candles and tested out the faucets. After a few minutes of rusty orange water spilling out into the tub and sink, they ran clear.

I went back to my suitcase to find soap and returned with several bottles that served as the only decorative items besides fake candles in the whole two rooms. I gathered my hair into a knot and dropped my clothes on the floor, shoving a stopper in the drain. I sank into the water, closing my eyes as it covered my face.

Maybe when I surfaced again, I would be happy, and not so lonely.

I emerged from my room in one of the dresses Mom had gotten for school. I found her in what was supposed to be the kitchen, swearing on the phone at the real estate agent who lied to us. I stopped and leaned against the arched entryway, smirking. At least she was done pretending. This irritated both of us.

"You should be fired, and then sent to Mortem!" Mom ended the call with a few more insults, and then sighed angrily.

"Nice one," I remarked, walking up to her. "Telling someone to go to hell on Earth."

"Pizzette, you need to watch your swearing. This isn't the city to talk like that." Mom studied my face, noticing the rivulets of water cascading down my neck from my wet and tangled hair. "You look like the definition of sadness."

"Damn, I thought I'd come pretty close to looking Cyan for a second." I blew out a breath, expecting it to lift my bangs. They stayed plastered to my forehead. "You know, being in this crappy mansion isn't helping my mood."

"Well, the prospect of you receiving a title should aid it. Don't you want to be a lady?" Mom ran her hand through my hair, the knots stopping her lithe fingers.

I did not want a title. I wanted to sit in a crowded outdoor shopping mall in Bark, sipping soda from a glass and laughing with my friends. Enjoying the sunshine, the absence of stares from being different, from being myself.

"Cyan is a beautiful country. I met your father here," Mom whispered as she untangled a clump of my hair.

My ears twitched. "I thought you never left Bark. You and Father lived here?"

"I lied to you. We were both born right here in the city." She paused. "So were you."

"You lied? I wasn't born in Bark?" Tears stung in my eyes. "I was an outsider in Bark all this time?"

"Pizzette, calm down. It was safer in Bark." She repeated the words in a perfect Cyan accent.

I stumbled backwards.

"We lived here for eight years. Left after the Burning," she explained in a mellow voice, the accent she had been hiding suddenly so clear in her words.

"Eight years?" The room was spinning, a sick pit settling in my stomach. Eight years was half my life, not the early period everyone left behind when they grew older. "How did I forget eight years?"

"We had your memory erased by a doctor, one who used to work at the palace. After your father died, I didn't want you to remember. I didn't want you to grow up missing him."

"My life has been a lie," I said flatly, crossing my arms. "And you never thought to tell me? You erased my memory? How?"

"I'm sorry. Things were dangerous then. I'll save the details for when you can understand."

I snorted. "The queen-to-be isn't even royal, and no one in this city cares. They take more offense when people from other parts of the world show up at their train station. They put more faith in their dressing than their smiles. And they apparently see nothing wrong with lying to their own children."

"Pizzette Marie-Rose Colfer." Mom finally gave up. She huffed furiously. "We need to get you looking and acting like a Cyan girl."

"What does that mean? According to you, I'm Cyan through and through."

"We're going shopping."

***

Petrakova woke up on top of a pile of folded newspapers. It was wet and smelled like old cement, but she was too frazzled to think about that. Her thoughts felt like a mess of tangled wires, and she did not have the presence of mind to clear it. Every thought came in bursts of clarity.

She was a runaway. The police were after her. Yesterday, she saw a rotating ad panel stop on an article with her name and picture on it. WANTED was typed in bold letters at the top.

She should not be found by the police. Something terrible was going on, and she was in the middle of it.

Petrakova slowly stood up, adjusting her pink satin dress that was unfortunately splattered with mud. She was hungry. Maybe she could run home and grab something before the police searched her home.

Then she would become a real fugitive. Cross Mudlark Moat, the old dried-out river, and make it to Pigladen. She would work for a farmer. Earn enough money to hire a real detective to find Marmi.

Her chest tightened, and she had to pinch her cheeks to keep from sobbing. *I can do this. I can find Marmi, and we can go back to our house again.*

She just had to believe in herself.

Petrakova slowly made her way through the back streets across the city. These were the turns and twists most folks pretended not to be familiar with.

Marmi always said everyone came from nothing, whether they wanted to admit it or not. Petrakova never understood her, but now was not the time to dwell on riddles. She could just see Marmi's small but spacious house over a couple rooftops.

She dove out of the protective cover of bushes and into the street. Smooth white cement slapped her soles. Her curls whipped her cheeks, and her breath came heavy and fast.

Most of the city's people were out doing afternoon activities, but Petrakova was apprehensive about using the traditional lock system. Instead, she lobbed a rock through a window and climbed through, the jagged edges biting into her sides.

Thud. She fell onto the hard washroom floor. For a minute, Petrakova held her head and squeezed her sobs down. Then she got up, wiped her cheeks, and grabbed a basket off the highest shelf she could reach.

The pantry and refrigerator were almost bare, but she stumbled upon a dry loaf of bread and smoked pork sausage. Petrakova continued her search, finding a small thermos she filled with water.

At the last second, she grabbed her blanket off her bed and Marmi's pearl bracelet from her bedroom.

Petrakova turned around and considered giving up for a second. *No. Be brave and find Marmi.*

She braced herself, and then threw open the front door and ran into the unknown.

***

Part 2

Mattie

Yesterday, Inger came into my lab screaming, *"Mattie. I need a test done,"* with a little glass tube in her hands.

The lab was glittering white. I had just finished scrubbing it down for the day. With a sigh, I put on my gloves and took the vial from her. It was full of hair.

"I need you to DNA test it. I think I may have found Isobel Lagarde."

That sent a chill down my spine. "Really?"

Lady Arabella, who came in behind her, harrumphed as I slowly untwisted the cap. I knew she hated me. She always had. She was the wife or widow or mistress of several wealthy men, strikingly beautiful with perfectly curled strawberry blonde hair. I did not come close to her in the looks department. I could always see my reflection in the glassware, and my messy red hair and dull blue eyes, did not compare to anyone's regal appearance. Lady Arabella thought a sixteen-year-old like me had no right to test DNA, let alone step inside the palace of Cyan.

I carefully immersed the hair strands in the testing solution while taking out the box that held Isobel Lagarde's nightcap's hair samples from the locker. I never thought I would need it, or at least, I never wanted to need it. They were preserved in a special solution, and for a moment, I wished something had gone wrong and we could not use them anymore. I poured both hair solutions into opposite sides of the tester, dread settling inside me.

"We can check tomorrow morning," I lied, knowing it only took a few minutes but wanting to lock up for the night.

Now we were back there again, all surrounding the machine and waiting for it to "finish."

"You know, Mattie designed Preserv," Inger said out of nowhere. "And she perfected using it to match DNA samples." She looked over at me, beaming. "She really improved the scientific field in Cyan. She's even better than the scientist we had before."

"Anyone can be better than that fool," Lady Arabella sneered.

I ignored her disinterest. I was Inger's prized servant after all.

It all started eight years ago. I fell ill at the orphanage and was sent to a nearby hospital when Inger happened to be passing through. She decided to take me back to Cyan City with her and the rest of her advisors at that time. Inger spent the years tutoring me in math and science, as though she believed I really had some talent in the area. Now, I was finishing projects the last palace doctor failed to do and developing more of my own.

Inger still left books and notes for me to learn from, but even now, I was not allowed to step inside Etiquette.

We could all wait in silence as long as they wanted to. I was used to being alone in here, refusing the radio Inger had offered to install on more than one occasion. It would have been a distraction, and I did not want to listen to anything that would remind me of the outside world. There was no need for music, movies, and advertisements relating to things I would not have time for as long as I lived here.

So, I stayed alone in silence, and tried not to think about everything I was missing.

I knew most girls my age wanted to explore the world and were far more ambitious than me. I was two years shy of adulthood, and traditionally expected to be just a little more adventurous and exciting. It was odd to stay indoors all the time, but it suited me for now. I just had to keep learning, keep doing these experiments for Inger so I had a place to live.

The machine chimed, snapping me out of my daydream. I had hit the lever without meaning to.

"We can give it more time for testing. I didn't mean to press the lever so early," I mumbled, trying to buy myself more time.

"Go on. It's already printed a data tag," Inger said quickly, erasing my options to delay.

Inger and Lady Arabella crowded around me as I pulled out the data tag with shaking fingers. I was not a slow reader, but this time, I had to give the results a second look to convince myself what I was seeing was true.

My voice quavered as I read the statement. "It's a match."

The atmosphere went from tense to choking and then to cloying all within one second.

I held the data tag, wondering if my eyes were deceiving me. Lady Arabella ripped the paper slip out of my hands and held it up to her face. "It's a match. Isobel Lagarde is alive."

"My niece is alive?" Inger sputtered without a shred of joy. "Petrakova is my niece?" She scrunched up her face and then swept her arm across the table, sending vials and test tubes to the ground. Precious spare samples were shattered and contaminated. Preserv soaked my slippers, squelching against my heels.

"No," I cried, diving down and trying to pick up the hair samples. I could not tell which pile of broken glass test tubes held which sample. "Madame, these were important DNA samples. They're all ruined."

A slap sounded against my cheek, vibrating my teeth and filling my mouth with fire.

Inger had slapped me.

"Be quiet, Mattie. Arabella and I need to speak in my office. Clean up this mess."

"Yes, Madame." My cheek burned as I filled a bucket with soapy water and grabbed a rag.

Inger and Lady Arabella walked out of the lab. I heard Lady Arabella scoff. "She's getting too old to be this stupid."

I threw the hair strands into an incineration chute. I was hoping the DNA data had been saved in a file. I could not soak up all the Preserv, so I simply wiped as much as I could with a gray towel. Soap splashed all over my knuckles and onto my sleeves.

Preserv, the solution I developed that prevented organic material from decaying. I imagined it soaking into my skin long enough. Me never growing old. Or maybe I would drink it and my body would stay young forever.

It was a fantasy. The solution was practically poison still. No one wanted to live forever. Not me, if it was with Inger in this palace.

But the dream was still strong in my mind.

I wrung the cloth again, soap and water running over my fingers. The mess was gone. The data tags sitting on the polished lab table, glaring and flagrant, reminding me that what I was doing was wrong.

I cursed, wishing I lied and tossed the tag to the side. Inger's reaction had not shown any compassion for this child. Inger would have her found and killed. The real princess was alive, and Inger did not accept that.

My technology and samples had found her. *My* adjustments to the pictures taken at her christening were nearly identical to the description the men at the police station had given.

Greedy pride swelled in my chest. Me. *Me*. Without *me*, Inger would still be searching for Isobel Lagarde.

But it would not be so simple. Her aunt already had no competition for the throne. Already, the people of Cyan did not care if she crowned herself or not. As long as they had their parties and fancy cars, the affairs of continuing an honest government did not matter.

With a sigh, I tied my hair back, locked my lab, and ran down the hall to Inger's office. I was rarely outside during the day, and the servants I passed were stunned by the redhead girl with freckles and muddy slippers who they scarcely saw.

I pressed my ear against the door, breathing carefully as I strained to catch their words.

"How are we going to find an eight-year-old in Cyan?" Lady Arabella asked in an icy voice.

"...probably in or around her home, wherever that is. If not, then she'll be in the woods, considering whether or not she decided to run away." Inger coughed, breaking up her lament. "I don't care where she is. I want her found and brought to the palace. And tell Jessica to take those pictures out of circulation before someone recognizes her and feels obligated to intervene."

"We should just end this before it becomes a problem," Lady Arabella said coldly. "No one has to see us smuggle in this girl and lead to more rumors."

"We can carry out more tests at the palace." Inger's suggestion seemed out of place. Did she want me to test her identity again? Double and triple check all the data? "Science has been known to fail."

"I say we leave the body in the gutter and move on. Open the Lagarde's virtual bank account again. We can try and hack it now that Jessica's girl is good enough."

"Or we can test Preserv," Inger chuckled, ignoring all of Lady Arabella's gruesome ideas. "We don't need the money yet. Why not have our fun with this one? It's been quite the chase."

"Whatever you say, Inger. I know the others are just itching to come back to the city."

I suddenly heard footsteps from inside walking in my direction. I covered my mouth with my palm and ran, leaving wet footprints in my path. Inger would know I eavesdropped.

I locked myself in the lab, trying to breathe evenly. *Clean something out, Mattie. Don't make anyone look twice. It's better that way.*

I never felt an obligation to like Inger, but she had sheltered me for so long. Seeing her true colors left me conflicted, wondering if there would ever be a better option for me.

As if. You're all alone in this world.

***

Luck

For two hours, Mama and I had been scouring the shops for Etiquette dresses, and I was stuck between two. It was almost a waste of time at this point, but after the flop that was my interview, I needed to be reminded that Etiquette was really happening.

We got a call a few minutes after returning home. Apparently, Inger was not having any more interviews. Everyone who applied by the deadline was accepted. I was bummed that the group was not handpicked anymore, but at least I would be at Etiquette in a week.

Next to Inger. The name sent chills down my spine. That would be the most unbearable part about all of this. Something about our leader had always bothered me.

"Lucienne, the white would be nice for dance lessons." Mama held up an ugly white dress with dangling bell sleeves. I shook my head.

"I want Princess Cyrana's lace, Mama. I want to have the prettiest lace in the whole school." A row of beautiful gowns hung on racks in the corner with low necklines, short sleeves, parted skirts, and matching pearly gloves. The lace was a replica of

Cyrana's lace. The late princess had a hobby for making armfuls of it, and when she passed, the best seamstresses in Cyan recreated the unique pattern.

I touched a delicate embroidered sleeve, tears welling in my eyes. *All we have left of the Lagarde family are some replicated dresses and photographs.*

"Oh! The green would go great with your eyes." Mama handed me two to try on, but I was still staring at the gown in my hands. I read the label carefully. *Original lace from the Recovery Foundation.*

"This one," I said quickly, pulling the hanger off the rack. "I want this one, Mama."

"That's rather expensive, Lucienne."

"Nothing is too expensive for me," I snapped, pulling the rest of the gowns apart to find one short enough for me. Instead of more gowns, I saw another face.

The girl was obviously from some lower system. She looked at the prices with wide eyes, and based on her dressing, she probably could not even count that high. Her cab-driving parents needed to get her out of my way. *She's so plain. Brown hair and eyes, and that dress is horrid.*

"Excuse me," I said.

"Excuse *me*," the girl said back, taking a gown off the rack and holding it against her body. Her head turned to the side. "Mom, I like this white one."

"Is that your size, Pizzette? The waist looks too large."

Mama, to my horror, went and introduced herself to the strangers. The girl was glaring at me. I tried to look mean in return.

"What are you and your daughter doing here?" Mama asked, her voice filled with fake friendliness. *That's right, Mama. Ask the good questions.*

I held back a laugh. They probably had no answer.

"We're getting Pizzette gowns to wear at Etiquette," the woman said back in the same tone.

My jaw dropped. Who were these people?

"We're doing the same. Lucky is only fourteen, two years younger than most entering students," Mama said with pride. "Her sister, three years older, is already in college."

"Well, Pizzette speaks two languages," the woman tried, sticking out her hand. "Edith Colfer. Nice to meet you."

"It's Elisabeth," Mama said in a tight voice. "Elisabeth Legrand."

Edith Colfer's eyes widened, and then she turned to her daughter, her voice almost mocking. "It looks like you and *Luck* will be great friends."

Mama and Edith kept talking, leaving Pizzette and I to exchange biting remarks.

I wrinkled my nose. "Where are you from? You look like you've spent your whole life working the fields."

"I'm from Bark, and no, I did not live on a farm." Pizzette turned her nose up, as if that intimidated me.

"You probably did. Is there dirt under your nails? Careful, you might stain the dress."

"No." She frowned, probably trying to come up with a smart response. She must have been about two years older than me and several inches taller, but that did not matter. I was not going to let her talk down to me, especially since she did not even belong here. "You're too short to even wear anything here."

"You're too poor. This is Princess Cyrana's lace. Do you know how much it costs?" I snorted. "I bet your farming family can't even afford it."

"My family owns a whole lot of diamonds," she spat, her hand closing around her necklace.

"Is that why you wear that hideous chain?" I left her with that insult and turned to go look at shoes. She did not follow me, which was perfectly fine.

I knelt down next to a display of handmade high-heeled boots, searching for the most expensive one before grabbing it off the shelf.

"Mom," Pizzette yelled like a ruffian, running down the aisle. "Let's go pay. We can't keep the chauffeur waiting."

Chauffeur? What was *she* talking about?

***

Pizzette

We had been living in Cyan for a week, and I was already looking forward to vacations far away from this dreary place. Mom's idea of a vacation was attending Etiquette's annual commencement gala for new and returning students. I spent the morning trying to convince her I was sick, but my cover was blown when she opened the door and found me circling routes out of the city on a map.

I did not want to go. I was plotting my escape while sitting in the back of a cab with Mom, who looked quite perplexed as she studied a map of the city, occasionally muttering things like, "They moved that shop?" and, "They spent money on a new fountain, there of all places?"

Snow fell, but somehow it was not as enchanting as I had expected it to be, since it hardly snowed in Bark. The ugly gray buildings and standoffish people made taking delight in anything seem childish. The driver's slow crawl was making us late and I was already exhausted.

The journey from Tumbleweed Gardens to the school gave me more than a glimpse of the city I had seen while inside the cab. The buildings, however ugly they were, reached the gray sky, towering overhead and making me feel very small. Shopping complexes took up entire streets, all overcrowded with traffic and people walking about, holding onto their parasols and shopping bags, and hurrying across crosswalks before the lights changed. Smoky food smells wafted down every path, all coming from dozens of high-end diners, restaurants, and bars, all busy in the evening. I could see people streaming in and out of open doors, some merry, others a little gloomy like me. The bars especially seemed to be alive with chaotic excitement. I could hear the music blasting from inside, teasing anyone who passed by with a taste of the world behind those blacked-out windows. I was only sixteen, and there was no way Mom would ever let me go anywhere in this city alone, but it was still nice pretending that all these places were open for me to explore. They, at least, seemed more interesting than a stuffy school full of stuck-up people like Luck.

When we finally arrived, I hurried into the palace ahead of Mom, holding my skirt off the ground and trudging through snow I guessed no one felt too obligated to shovel.

I had ditched the Cyrana-lace-thing for one of my old dresses with a parted skirt and crinkly, stepped-on train. My jet-black gloves went up to my elbows and left my hands looking lean and dangerous. My hair was braided with dried flowers that smelled old and stale, surrounding me with a very unapproachable aura. *Make fun of me, Cyan aristocrats. I dare you.*

Two guards whose faces both looked the same and completely different led me inside without hiding their disdain. "The serving staff uses the door to the left."

"I'm here to dance," I said, mimicking their accent. "And I'm one of the Etiquette girls."

There was not even a semblance of approval on their faces. "Go in using the right door."

"*Merci.*" I pushed the heavy door out of my way and followed some of the other girls down a winding path into the ballroom, leaving Mom to her own devices. The rest of the palace we passed through was shrouded in shadows and billowy curtains, and since I was not looking for ghosts, I did not stray.

The ballroom was filled with lace, bright gowns, and wine everywhere, even in the hands of people my age. Girls were spinning circles around me with their dance partners, the music a tangible force compelling them to dance, to move.

For a moment, I wanted to go and watch the orchestra while eating finger-foods, but someone tapped my shoulder. It was a red-headed boy holding a tray of small glasses.

"What is this?" I asked, picking one up before he could offer me any.

"Pearl liquor. Well, I'm telling people it's punch, but they don't care either way," he replied, tipping the tray toward me. "Take another, love. You look like you could use some."

I did, quickly swallowing both before he thought I was too scared to. It burned going down, but I resisted the urge to cough. "It's not too bad, and I'm fine. I don't like big crowds, that's all."

"You can hide in them, be anyone you want," he said, taking the two glasses and dropping them in his extra-large pockets. "No one looks too closely at anyone here."

"Yeah. I get the feeling that no one cares." The liquor part was making my heart hurt a little less, so I took another glass. A fourth.

"Well there's someone out there." He took the fourth and set it back on the tray, smirking coquettishly. "I was only trying to cheer you up, not render you unable to stand."

"Thanks, but I think I needed that last one and a dozen more to make it through the semester." I looked up into his blue eyes, and my head started to spin. "And two bottles for the next."

"Pizzette," Mom yelled from a few tables over, having finally found me. "Let's take a picture."

"You should go." He took the empty glass from my hands, giving me a sympathetic smile. "It won't be this way forever."

***

Mattie

Inger had spent the last couple minutes walking back and forth between her office and the lab, forgetting something in each and then yelling at me until she remembered where it was.

"Mattie, I'll be leaving in two minutes to make my appearance at the gala. Swab those test tubes and finish that human Preserv sample. You've had more than enough time, and I outlined the procedure for you, so it shouldn't be hard."

That was easy for her to say. I kept my head down over my pad and paper, trying to understand the mystery of Preserv. Inger had recently uncovered notes written by someone trying to create a similar serum, but theirs contained more ingredients than the Preserv I had doctored. I still could not quite understand what the *Energy Replacement* and *Artificial Skill Pattern* were supposed to be or how I was supposed to find them. Whoever wrote these notes, and subsequently erased out all signs of their identity, was trying to fool me. I doubted any of this was real. A preserving serum that was safe enough to be consumed by a living subject. That didn't sound possible.

"Inger, I just don't understand how to make this. The Preserv I finished last night might be fine if ingested, but these ingredients aren't found in my databases, and the elemental structure isn't on the charts."

Inger stopped in the middle of searching her purse to stare at me. "Are you really stopping there? Don't you know how to discover anything?"

"It's not as easy as simply combining some chemicals. Replicating a genetic pattern that I've never seen before with limited equipment in these conditions is next to impossible." I put down the notebook, giving my eyes a rest. "I can keep looking in the morning, but right now, I have no idea where to start."

"Are you going to know tomorrow?" Inger asked, finding her perfume bottle and dousing herself.

"I can't guarantee that."

"Then what's the difference between tomorrow and today? You might as well spend the same amount of time thinking about those impossible things. Did anyone ever make it anywhere in the world by waiting? The only thing that changes tomorrow is how many days you wasted, and I'm not waiting a decade to have this Preserv to myself." She slammed her purse down on the lab table, looking for something else again.

I hated to argue with Inger. She was loud and abrasive, and I was the complete opposite. "I need time to think about this too. It's not like no one ever had idle time."

"That's the problem with all these Cyan people," Inger muttered, turning the pockets inside-out. "They're all so lucky they don't have to worry about time. Everyone is, to be honest."

I opened the notebook again, annoyed that I had given up so easily.

"And there you go, just doing what I say all the time. God, obedience is a virtue, but you make it something else." Inger withdrew a folded paper, scanning both sides before slipping it into her sleeve. "No one wants to do anything for themselves anymore. You're all lazy."

"I don't think so—"

"Then figure it out. What if I told you the answer had nothing to do with your little theorems and formulas? This is the biggest scientific mystery of time, simply because you can't explain it with science. Sure, there are genes, but the rest of it, the *artificial* part, is something else entirely. I hope you'll do your best to understand." She gathered up her things and left the lab, slamming the door closed.

I knew better than to follow her out. Instead, I went back to reading, trying to make sense of the words, or at least follow Inger's advice and stop trying to connect it with everything I had ever learned.

Whoever the old scientist was, they could not have based their research on fallacies. I had to figure out the puzzle they left in their wake.

***

Luck

There were snowflakes in my hair and tears frozen on my cheeks. The blue lace of my gown pooled out beneath me like a river, swathing my legs in fabric and hiding them from the snowstorm. The pounding music leaked outside through the cracked-open door, floating over the steps like a trail of wind. From inside, I could hear laughter and merriment, and here I was crying.

It was all hitting me now. Tomorrow, Mama and Papa would leave me on the stone steps of Etiquette and drive away. I would not be home again for two years, except on scant holidays. And after, I would become a lady royal and spend years serving the throne of Cyan. Home was a faint memory now, and I was afraid I was going to forget it too soon.

I finally managed to quieten my sobs, chastising myself for losing control. Maude was already in college. Leaving home was not supposed to make you cry. I should have been excited. *Come on, Luck. You're better than that.*

But my eyes were teary and my mind telling me the opposite. I wanted to stay home and be a child for a few days more.

My curls tickled my cheek as I bent over to put my glass slippers back on. A salty drop rolled off my nose, splashing on the smooth surface.

The slippers were a going-away gift from Papa.

Instead of returning to the party, I walked into the courtyard away from the domineering guards who had not bothered to ask why I was upset.

Two figures beneath a distant tree caught my eye. I stopped where I stood, smothering a gasp.

Papa was with another woman.

I swiveled around, too disgusted to keep looking. *Don't start drawing conclusions. Maybe she's a friend...*

The yelling, the arguments, and the letters Polly found...

Just turn away and keep walking. You don't want to make a scene now, with everyone watching.

I took a step back, my glass slipper catching in the snow. "Ah!" I lost my balance, spinning around and falling in the snow.

"Who's there?" Papa shouted.

Nice going, Luck. You just had to go be a little sneak, right? I rolled over, crawling forward and behind the tree, ignoring the cold snow biting into my forearms.

"Do we need to get out the checkbook?" *Who is that? Do I know that voice?*

I hunched over behind the tree, covering my mouth with my hands.

This was ridiculous. Why couldn't I just stop being childish and talk to my own father? Why was I hiding?

"It's better if no one finds out about this…us, for a while. With Lucienne being accepted at such an early age and Maude joining the class studying in Gallen."

What is he talking about? I covered my face with my hands, shivering. Ideas were starting to come to my mind, but I did not want to consider any one of them.

He was getting closer, the footfalls lost in the snow.

Such pretty snow. I used to make snow angels with Maude when we were younger. Two each so we had a family of four. *Us four.*

No. Why am I thinking of our family like that?

"Whoever you are, we need to have a discussion," Papa called, his voice hardening. It was clear that he was on the other side of the tree, that stranger no longer by his side. "You just have to agree to be very quiet."

Oh, I can do that. I'll be so quiet, only after you answer my questions.

"There's no reason to hide," he said. "I know you're standing right there."

I yelped as he rounded the tree, grabbing my arm. He was just as surprised as me.

"Luck, what the hell are you doing outside?"

***

Pizzette

Mom split after taking two pictures, so I entertained myself, circling the ballroom and stealing little treats from different tables to avoid looking like a pig. Some people here were so fake, pretending the cakes and chocolates were not delicious and leaving an abundance left over.

Where was that guy with the drinks? If this gala lasted any longer than a few hours, I was going to need a whole lot of that stuff to forget every minute.

I did another lap around the ballroom, not having any luck. He had probably gone inside the kitchen or something. *He's working, idiot. He doesn't cater only to you.*

I looked over my shoulder before swiping two more strawberry tarts, trying not to be disappointed. Apparently, Inger was about to address the audience, and it was mandatory to pay attention. There were chairs lining the ballroom, obviously not enough for the crowd. I would have to fight for a pair of seats. *Mom, we're about to lose our good viewing spots.*

I started for the doors, wondering if she had gone out for some quiet. I opened the door, and a second later someone grabbed my wrist, making me jump back.

"Pizzette, it's just me," Mom said quickly, moving out of the way so the people coming in behind her had enough room to pass.

"Where did you go?"

"Don't mind me…Oh, is that jam on your dress?"

Someone came bounding in behind her. A man was holding that wench, *Lucienne*, by her ear. Her gown was wet across the back.

"What's going on?" I asked, batting her hand off my wrist. "You can't disappear and then show up like nothing happened. I needed someone to talk to. I don't have friends here, remember?"

Mom pushed me toward the throng of dancers, her attention elsewhere. "Then go make some."

Luck stepped on my shoe as she stomped past me, distancing herself from the man who was probably her father.

Mom and the man walked away at the same time, leaving us alone.

***

The joyous atmosphere had left the ballroom. People still swayed to the music, but I could not feel the beat or enjoy myself and my desserts.

I had too much on my mind. I leaned against the back of a chair, waiting for Inger's address so we could leave. Where was that boy with the liquor? Other servers had come and gone, but he still did not make an appearance. The drinks were making me feel sick, but at least they made me think I was happy for a few minutes.

I had questions for everyone, about my memory, the strange man, this entire isolated ghost town of a city.

Why? Why did Mom never tell me who we were?

A hush fell over the ballroom. I looked up at the gallery above the floor, draped in curtains matching the Cyan flag and lined with guards. At the center was the woman from the television on the train; Inger Kaleon.

The queen-to-be was fit into a maroon gown with an elegant black rose petal veil. The roses travelled up the back of her gown, running over one shoulder and up into the veil she was wearing over her mousy brown hair. From a distance, with her chin lifted and standing above everyone, she looked regal, but there was something lacking about her presence, something in the way the entire room suddenly felt cold.

Everyone around me curtsied in unison, and I dropped down before Inger noticed.

"Hello, my bright, shining stars," she began in a saccharine voice.

***

Inger gazed over the balcony at the new Etiquette class. The ladies were definitely excited, though she could not fathom why. Perhaps it was those titles everyone salivated over while their servants polished silver headdresses a few feet away.

Lady Arabella was amongst the support crew hidden behind a wall of guards. Inger choked after her greeting; the view of the ballroom too reminiscent of memories she wanted to bury. For the first time in her eight years of doing this, looking at the floors she had once danced upon gave her a knot in her stomach.

Lady Arabella reached between two guard's arms and poked Inger's shoulder. "Don't think, just talk. It's not like those people down there know how to do either."

Inger chuckled, and then rolled her shoulders back. *Queen. You're already the ruler. Convince them you earned it after all those years behind Cyrana.*

"Tonight, we are going to celebrate the last day of your childhood. You will become ladies and receive land grants and a title to match your new status. Etiquette was completed eight years ago, a project started by my late sister, *Princess* Cyrana Lagarde." Inger pursed her lips, the uneasy feeling sticking around. "I see some of you are wearing the lace she designed."

Several of the girls giggled and flounced their gaudy skirts, beside themselves because *Madame* Inger had noticed them. The whole display made Inger want to slap someone.

Cyrana, how I abhor your name.

"Etiquette is my personal project, the late Lagardes' monument to the world." Inger pretended to shudder, earning some sympathy from the girls who were sensible enough to stop ogling over themselves and pay attention. *Always spoiled, Cyan. Every generation is a worse version of Garnet.* "And yes, I said late."

It was finally quiet. Somewhere in the back, two trays of glasses clinked together.

"I will be accepting the crown of Cyan soon. My private unit has unanimously appointed me, and as there is no opposition from the public at this moment…" She smiled, pulling the veil out of her eyes. It felt so good to have people paying attention to her in this ballroom again. "I am to be crowned Queen Inger Kaleon of Cyan in a few weeks."

***

The palace grounds were alive with music and lights, the gala lasting into the early hours of the morning. It was truly the night intended to give the next generation of Cyans one last chance to let out childish antics and concerns, leaving them too exhausted the next morning to even dread going to school. It was almost like a rite of passage, and although similar parties happened all around the country, the grandest would always be celebrated in the Lagarde's castle.

The city was a whole other story at night. The evils people liked to pretend did not exist were so obvious. Maybe that was why every young girl and boy was supposed to have a curfew. Parents would not want them staggering home drunk and covered in trash because they wandered out of their little bubble into the real city.

The trash collectors only drove around at night, since the darkness was kind enough to obscure identities for free. They zipped past storefronts overflowing with wasted food half-spoiled and half-poorly preserved, an acceptable meal for the beggars that came in from the outskirts of the city, frequenting the bars and cheap diners to haggle for change and scraps. Really, it was a lovely sight if one would be so generous as to forgive the rest of the city for being so old and formal and respectful, as long as it was daylight.

In the dark of night with slushy snow crowding the forest floor, Petrakova had not expected to get any sleep, not with the scary sounds coming from the city and the cold her blanket could not protect against. She sat down against a tree trunk, pulling her legs up to her chin and trying to focus on breathing slowly. Staying warm. Finding Marmi.

Almost a week out here, and she was not any closer to finding her. Disappointment was the worst emotion to lose consciousness with.

A few hours later, she woke up because someone was trying to kidnap her.

The stranger grunted, throwing Petrakova against the hard ground. The man fell flat on his back, swearing under his breath.

She rolled over quickly, the log the man had tripped on just out of reach. She vaguely remembered it being several feet away.

"Get away from me!"

The man swore again, his dirty hand covering her mouth. He feigned an apology.

"I didn't see that you were so small. I thought you were some runaway."

Petrakova crawled backwards, not letting her guard down. She could not trust anyone after the police had betrayed her. "That's not true." She hid her hands behind her back, pressing her fingernails into her palms.

"Why don't you tell me your name? Kids your age should be at home, not in the cold." The man reached forward, his rough hands mingling through her black curls.

Petrakova waited for his hand to move, taking a few steps away while he closed the gap between them. "None of your business, that's what it is."

The man sighed, letting his hand fall to his side. He looked almost disappointed. "I don't suppose you remember me. I was at your christening."

"What?" Petrakova did not have a moment to react. The man jerked her wrists behind her back, tying them with thick ropes.

"I've got her, Inger. I'll be back within the hour," he said to no one.

Was he with the police? Had they found her?

Petrakova swooned, the forest blurring around her. The city's flagrant noise and all of its excitement turned to nothingness as she hit the ground, something pricking her upper arm.

There was no one around to hear her if she even dared to scream.

It was too late for that anyway. She was suddenly exhausted and could barely keep up with what was happening.

The man picked her up. He was taking her away.

No. I need to find Marmi.

"Right. Yeah, I made sure I wasn't followed."

Let me go. I have to find my mother.

Petrakova opened her eyes, and for half a second, she almost felt she was strong enough to send the whole forest crashing down on the stranger, but just as quickly, the fight left her, and she was out.

***

Part 3

Mattie

I was dancing down a winding hall, light as a feather and graceful like a swan. My gown was made of the finest lace, and my soft hands were gloved in satin. A smile painted itself across my face, and at the last moment I looked over my shoulder. I saw myself standing alone in a corner, eight years old again, with my head in my hands, bored as I looked at the palace where I would be working soon. A younger Inger stood behind me, her face as placid as it has always been.

"This is the next phase of your life, Matilda. Don't make me go through all that trouble again."

The stool I was sitting on tipped backwards. I barely caught myself before hitting the ground. *It was just a dream.* I had fallen asleep poring over the old scientist's notes, still confused over where the Energy Replacement and Artificial Skill Pattern originated from, but I found a piece of the puzzle. It looked like the scientist was studying the Traits observed in people, the physical or elemental additions that made them slightly less human and more mythical. Some even called them powers. Luckily for us Cyan folk, we had never seen someone walking around with two sets of eyes or hypersensitive ears. *Yet.*

I stood up and yawned. I still did not see the connection with Preserv, but at least their research had a motive.

It was the first day of classes at Etiquette. I might as well not show up disheveled and dusty.

I left everything where it was and walked to my chamber, locking myself in my private bathroom. Everything here was a gift from Inger, and despite how cold she could be, it was a generous accommodation, especially for someone as lowly as me. It was a guest suite for nobles really, with more than enough room for one person, still plain since I had never decorated it.

I emerged from the bathroom clean, no longer smelling like chemicals. I lingered on my hair, braiding it and twisting it up into a bun on top of my head. I chose my nicest dress from the selection Inger had ordered for me and found matching slippers.

I felt silly, but I did not want to bump into anyone from Etiquette looking like the miserable person I was.

The palace was livelier than I had seen it in years. Cameras were at the ready, snapping pictures of ladies and interviewing first-year students so excited they rambled through every question. Journalists lined the corridors, sipping coffee the servants brewed at miraculous speeds and passed around. The yard connecting the palace to the school was occupied by more reporters and families who had come to drop off their daughters.

I weaved through the crowd, wanting to disappear. I did not know what it felt like to hug my parents goodbye.

"Matilda!" Inger's voice cut across the courtyard. I whipped my head around to find her. "I need your help." She was standing in an arched entry to the palace, impatient as ever.

I crossed the courtyard, surprised when I heard a camera shutter go off.

"And who might you be, miss?" a reporter asked, his entire crew turning around to film my face.

"Oh, I'm just…"

"*Lady* Matilda. You have two more seconds," Inger called again, saving me from revealing my lame self to the entire world.

"Exactly what she said," I murmured, gathering my skirt in my hands and running towards her.

***

"I have given you a title," Inger said out of nowhere as she and I walked to the dining room away from the crowd.

I sat in one of the gilded chairs, my heart hammering in my chest. I tried folding my hands to hide my tremors.

"Why would you do that?" I asked, trying not to stare as a trio of servants brought out breakfast just for us.

"You have been working hard in the lab." Inger uncovered her tray and I copied her, my stomach growling when I saw the large slices of toast and eggs with three types of jam, all for me. Even though I was like Inger's personal scientist, she had given me almost everything but love. I raided the kitchen and argued with the staff for food. Rarely had Inger ever remembered I needed sleep and water in addition to the clothes and room. Still, it was a gift to even live here, and not in some run-down orphanage in Pigladen.

"Thanks." I felt the corners of my mouth turning up. Maybe Inger was finally warming up to me.

"Lady Matilda, Royal Advisor to the future queen. You're part of my team now. Expect the guards to start following you around too." Inger dug into her breakfast, her attention mostly on the food.

I nibbled on a piece of toast, suddenly feeling guilty. "What about Isobel?"

Inger reached across the table and grabbed my chin, pulling me to my feet. I bumped into the table, knocking over several teacups.

The servants stared at her, horrified. "Madame!"

"Leave," Inger hissed. They tripped over their feet to obey her, leaving us alone.

"You are an idiot, Mattie. What if they heard more? Do you not understand that finding Isobel last night is not joyous news?" Inger growled, letting go of my face.

"Sorry…" I rubbed my jaw, wincing. "Why not let her rule? She's the rightful heir. We could be restoring a lost monarch."

"It's called politics," Inger snapped. "You do your work for me, and you do not ask questions."

I nodded, hoping my face would not bruise. I held back my tears, knowing she would only become more enraged if I lost it completely and started to cry in front of her.

"Sorry. I really am."

"Do you realize a title does not make you a princess or anyone special? You told the cameras Madame Inger gave you a title. You let them see your face and hear the admission. That means if the secret gets out and people hate me, they're going to hate you. It's a game. If I lose, you lose with me."

"Okay," I whispered, my voice nearly gone. "I understand." Who was I to think she was trying to help me out? We were the same as we had always been.

"Then sit down and finish eating. We have to go and welcome the students. The sooner, the better. All these cameras are making me claustrophobic."

***

Pizzette

I wore a short yellow dress with puffy sleeves and a childish headband, loving how unruly my hair looked and how plain my slippers were. As one final act of rebellion, I had decided not to dress for the cameras. They would not see me enter with anything but a smug look on my face and a large diamond hanging off my neck.

Mom waved until I could no longer see her. The driver eased the cab through the frozen mud, neatly cresting the hill without sliding back and killing us both.

This driver was more agreeable than the last one we used, but I still kept quiet, mostly because I was trying to memorize the city before I was locked away in school. It was morning, and the streets were full of cars and pedestrians, all on their way to work and the stores. I wondered what it was all our wealthy neighbors did to stay afloat, but after seeing so many slovenly-dressed people scrambling across intersections, I figured that some ancestor had done the work a couple centuries ago, and their descendants were enjoying the money now, without a care in the world. I guess if you were in possession of several million cizotes, there was no rush to put more in the bank, as if it would run out anytime soon. I could only wonder how so many people could remain idle all day, leaving home to shop and returning to parties and dinners and banquets. Take out all the lights and dresses and wine, and it seemed like a pretty repetitive and boring life to live from my side.

Soon, the cab blended into the procession entering the palace's bounds, locking away the rest of the city.

I found myself stuck to the windows, nevertheless, trying to see through the hordes of white, gold, and lace, which even the poorest people could flaunt. I looked down at my bare knees with a smirk. I was the only girl showing so much skin here, especially in the middle of winter. Talk about a lasting impression.

I traced the filigree surrounding my father's diamond, smiling faintly. *It's just you and me now. We're going to a whole other planet called Etiquette Boarding School.*

I thanked the driver and exited the cab. My legs immediately froze, and I almost regretted not covering up. My cloak was at the bottom of my bag, and since I was committed to my protest, I left it there.

The driver kindly carried my bags through the snow as I followed the stream of students heading for the double doors leading into the school. I could see Madame Inger over their heads, dressed in a dark blue gown and black ermine cloak looking like she was doing something important. There was a girl about my age standing next to her with a circlet made of silver nestled in her hair. She was pretty enough to scheme herself into any baron's bed, which I suspected happened a lot here.

Inger's short nose wrinkled as her eyes swept the crowd, disapproving. I stood up straighter as she began to speak.

"Hello students and future ladies of Cyan. I am accompanied by Royal Advisor, Lady Matilda, to welcome you to the school of Etiquette."

Lady Matilda offered a small wave to the crowd. The sleeves of her gown quivered a bit when she moved less than an inch away from Inger. It was a slight movement, but I knew it stood for something.

We were led out of the cold and into what looked more like a vacation palace than a school. My dress was receiving some disgusted looks, but I ignored it, too captivated by the grandeur of the school.

We entered an enormous room filled with circular tables surrounded by white chairs. "This is the dining hall," Inger announced, now joined by several guards. A few followed Lady Matilda as well. "Meals are served four times a day; breakfast at six, lunch at twelve, dinner at seven, and desert at seven thirty."

I nodded to myself, wondering if there was a snack bar to get me through the waiting periods. With this kind of schedule, I would starve before my next meal.

"Most of the classrooms are upstairs. Dorms begin to the right and span the entire right wing of the building, some on the second and third levels. We also have recreation rooms on this floor, a dance studio, gym, and swimming pool downstairs." Inger looked back at us, bored. "We will be taking a trip to the Sea of Cyan in a few days as a way to welcome the new term."

The sea I was supposedly born next to. I was getting closer and closer to home, and still remembered nothing.

***

Mattie

I programmed scanners for every room several days ago. The hallways were filled with their mechanical voices asking for people's identities, and the chatter of excited students. Inger and I watched luggage roll by and ladies excitedly touring their suites for the first time.

"Did you figure out the notes I left you?" Inger whispered.

"Somewhat. It seems as though the scientist was trying to mimic the abilities of people with Traits. There are several chemical substitutes they might have experimented with. I just can't figure out what that has to do with Preserv." I picked at the circlet on my head, wondering how long it would be until Inger asked for it back. I guess if I was to be seen in public, I had to play the part as well. I was still fuming over what she'd said over breakfast, but I was in no position to do anything now. Maybe not ever, as long as I was always stuck next to her.

"They were probably chasing immortality as something they were not," Inger muttered, her eyes darkening. "Can you finish it soon?"

"I'll try to make the solution into pills, but I need human subjects to test it on." I blinked several times, wishing I had kept my progress to myself. "I mean, the dosages still need to be calculated before I go that far, and I ought to try it on myself to be fair."

"No. Don't go down that road. I'll find a subject, just keep working." Inger walked away, her guards following like dogs.

I turned without a word, feeling the eyes of some of my fake guards on me. They were really kind, but I needed them to leave me alone.

"I have to go back to the palace now. I don't need to play it up for the cameras once I'm inside," I said, feeling bad for turning them away.

One of them, a young man with intoxicatingly blue eyes responded. "As you wish, Lady Matilda."

"You should really call me Mattie," I said, holding up a hand. "You know it's all for show."

He looked bashful for a second, and then one of the higher-ups spoke for him.

"Don't mind Tomas. It's all out of respect, Lady. We'll take you inside."

"Thank you." After today, I would probably never see them again, so I tried to save mental pictures of their faces. It was a waste of effort, since my memory had never been dependable. Still, I appreciated their company as we trekked across the courtyard again, now vacant and ghostly without the cameras and noise.

To my surprise, the shy one, Tomas, offered me his arm.

"I'll escort you, Lady," he said in a low voice, speaking only so I could hear. "Only if you'll accept."

I nodded, ignoring the racing of my heart as he led me back inside, both of us followed by the team of guards, like we were starlets on our way to a premiere. It was a silly thing to imagine, but I had to think of something to keep from blushing and tripping in front of everyone.

Despite my worrying, there was *someone* by my side who I knew would not let that happen to me. *Because it's his job. Nothing else. Oh, now you're smiling, and it looks strange because no one said anything.*

Oh well. Everything happy and light always ended so quickly.

The guards left me before I entered the lab. I stayed there for a few minutes, the high I had been feeling fading away. I was still alone, and my temporary companions had already gone.

I guess not everyone had a way to fill the hole inside their heart.

I could go back to work, or maybe… I could try and find Isobel before Inger ruined her life.

***

Luck

The lump in my throat refused to budge as the cab approached Etiquette and I saw coaches belonging to other families leaving. I did not know I would feel so lonely once my solo ride left Tumbleweed Gardens.

Maude left earlier that day for Principles without a heartfelt goodbye, far too excited since her trip had been moved up earlier. I was already looking forward to our first break around Christmas.

Mama and Papa slept through my departure, or rather, kept their door closed all morning. I asked Tor to tell them I loved them before I left. It would not sound the same coming from our middle-aged cook, but it was better than nothing.

I smoothed the sleeves of my gown again, the wrinkles refusing to fade. The bright red fabric stood out against my pale skin. I had picked out several of the tight-fitting and frilly-skirted gowns, hoping no one else would be bold enough to wear such a style. The ends of my light hair were painted orange which would fade in less than a day. I still had to make a good impression. Even if I arrived alone, I did not have to look scared and small.

I did not speak to the driver when we joined the line entering the compound. He was my sole temporary companion, but I had nothing to say to him.

You don't need anyone to idolize you, Luck. You just have to become what you love and accept that not everyone is going to care.

Despite my pep talk, once we stopped inside the courtyard, my anxiety skyrocketed. I was frozen, my arms as cold as the snow.

The driver wordlessly passed me my cloak from the trunk, dropping the rest of my boxes on the ground. I wrapped myself with it, wishing Maude was sitting next to me. Someone.

Mama and Papa fighting. Papa with that other woman. Suddenly I was sobbing, my tears freezing as they came. He had told me it meant nothing, *promised,* but I found it hard to believe.

I covered my face with my hands so the driver and any onlookers would not see my weakness. *I'm too scared, I just want to go back home...*

Don't be a coward, Lucienne. Sit up straight and open the door smiling. Who are you supposed to be?

Two minutes later, I was composed, my eyes dry.

"Lady Lucienne, it is time for you to get out," the driver said, opening the side door.

I took a deep breath, then stepped out beaming.

***

We had ten minutes to unpack our belongings and return to the dining hall.

I told the driver to leave before I lost my patience with their incessant talking and walked in alone. The suite was massive, fully furnished with a sofa by the window for reading and a television and computer on the cherrywood desk. The closet was vast and had another window, the shelves and racks bare. I almost regretted dismissing the driver when I started lifting my dresses out of the suitcases and laid them on the floor. The process of hanging each one was going to hurt my shoulders. I was not used to doing much around the house.

I gave up after a few minutes and stalked back to the bedroom. My silk duvet and sheets from home did not even stretch across the whole mattress, and I had not even begun to unload my toiletries in the bathroom.

Don't start crying, Luck. I walked into the bathroom and turned on the water. It was as cold as the snow outside but felt nice against my skin. I pressed my chilled hands against my cheeks, waiting for my eyes to stop burning. *This isn't so bad.*

There was always something happening at the manor. Servants vacuuming, Maude down the hall to talk to if I was bored. Mama and Papa too, when they were not working. Here, I knew no one.

I tried putting on the bed sheet again for fifteen minutes, fighting with the fitted disaster until I threw it at the wall. *Stupid sheets probably shrank when Polly dried them.*

I left the room, locking it by scanning my palm. I hesitated for a moment, the sight of clusters of friends and strangers heading to the dining hall nerve-wracking. I hated to feel left out, which was why it was easier to stay home. I had not gone to public school in years, and my only companion now was my own imagination.

Lady Royals don't hesitate.

I forced myself to step into the hallway. I was not going to graduate behind everyone else. I had to keep my chin up and make sure everyone saw me.

***

Pizzette

I was too good at making myself the outcast. The crowd was thinner around me wherever I walked, which I would just have to get used to. It was not the fault of the others; it just seemed my antics had no place in this world, and it was starting to show.

Inger returned to stand before the throng of restless students. She raised her hand, and the chatter stopped.

"Hello ladies. You will need to be assigned class schedules and link your tuition to your virtual accounts. To make this as orderly as possible, stand in line and be ready to provide your name and account information."

I curtsied along with everyone else, but my skirt came nowhere close to the ground.

I fiddled with my diamond as I merged into the line. I ignored the meaningless conversation around me and confined myself to my thoughts.

Dwelling on the fact that I was Cyan made me sick. There were eight years of my life missing from my memory, and according to Mom, they had been removed by some faceless, nameless doctor from the palace. I did not understand how, but as far as I was concerned, there was no scar along my hairline or spontaneous unexplained headaches to base my hypothesis on.

I ran my hand through my hair, fingers dancing along my scalp. Nothing. No bumps or scars or bald patches. It was a mystery no one was going to uncover for me.

A shiver ran up my back. The line had continued without me.

I peeked over my shoulder. There were at least eighty girls behind me, and the front was not really taking off yet. No one would notice if I slipped away for a few minutes.

I simply walked off in search of the library Inger had left out of her detailed description of the school. Maybe she assumed none of us liked to read.

Etiquette really owed its charm to its old-fashioned French doors and décor, and Europian building layout. The classrooms were large with windows or skylights in each one. I poked my head into a few, noticing the absence of light switches and the presence of candles and real fireplaces in their place. The standing desks were adjustable, fitted at the back with head and elbow rests for people with lazy posture, like mine. The floors were polished cherry wood and acacia wood which grew in abundance around the city, probably to obey the Environment Restoration Act. The place smelled like it was fresh out of nature, as though I was walking through a forest.

I smiled a little. I would not mind feeling like I was outside.

My search of the two upper floors revealed no library. Without any thought for punishments here, I skipped down the staircases and right out the front door. There were a couple guards stationed outside, but I threw my shoulders back and walked like I was supposed to be leaving. They left me alone.

For two seconds.

"Lady, where are you going?"

I looked him straight in the eyes, pretending I was not cold, and half scared. "I'm going to the palace. There is some information I need to look up at the library." *Gosh, I hope there's a library there.*

"We'll escort you inside." The guard walked ahead of me, nodding to one of his partners. "Give the lady your coat, Clint."

"Why, thank you," I said quietly as the guard called Clint draped his jacket over my shoulders. It was lighter than I had expected and far too big, but it was warm.

I walked into the palace surrounded by my own private guards, fooling anyone who looked into thinking I belonged. Clint offered to take me to the library, and the rest of the guards hung back. I had not been so observant, but I glanced back before entering the library and saw about a dozen more filtering in and out of the halls.

"You'd think someone really important lived here," I said under my breath.

"Madame Inger."

"Oh, you have ears." I covered my face with my hands, mortified. "Forget I said that. I will pay you."

Clint's amber eyes became mischievous, a striking expression for such a serious face to make. "What did you say?"

"Thanks." I strolled ahead of him, hoping he would give me a little privacy now that we were surrounded by bookshelves. The layout of the library was simple enough, with dozens of uniform shelves towering overhead, teeming with books, scrolls, and old-fashioned newspapers that weren't on a screen. I still had no clue where to start though, so I pretended to be very interested in some gardening books while he stood a few feet away. "You don't have to keep guarding me."

"I actually do. It's my job." Clint looked like he was smiling, so I chuckled back. "You seem confused."

"How did you know?"

"You're holding that book upside down."

"Oh. I'm really good at pretending." I set the book back in place, hoping I could trust him to keep quiet. "Okay, I'm actually looking for information on this doctor who used to work at the palace. I figured there'd be a journal or some record I could read."

"Really? Here I was thinking you were looking for some fanciful literature."

I raised my eyebrows, surprised someone with such a serious face knew how to joke around. "Do you know their name or where I can find them?"

"Lady, you did not have permission to leave Etiquette, did you?" Clint's eyebrows lifted in mock surprise. "Are you a spy?"

"Heavens no. At least, not for Cama or something." I shrugged. "You didn't answer me."

"That man left about seven years ago. I think he lives somewhere in the city, but he's rarely at the palace or his office at the hospital." Clint threw his arm over my shoulder, turning me around. "Now let's head back before Madame Inger comes out screaming and fires me."

"You have to tell me his name at least."

"Ah…Cadmire or something like it. Yes, Dr. Cadmire. It's a name you hear in the wind around here." Clint guided me back through the doors and into the hallway.

I had not been paying much attention before, but I was sure the guards waiting for us were completely different from the ones before.

"It's time to go to class, lady," Clint said, his voice serious again. "You don't want to make a bad impression on the first day."

***

Mattie

I finally understood it.

The scientist was studying the genetic code that created Trait variations in humans. The old scientist had come to the conclusion that Trait genes needed to match very specifically to create a gifted person. Whatever caused the integration into much of the population was caused by something even more complex than epigenetics. I was surprised the scientist had come to such cohesive conclusions.

 This side of the world was notorious for its stark contrasts in genetics by country. Traits were practically absent from Cyan. However, the scientist thought that if they could take a sample of a Trait from a real source and enhance it with chemically engineered agents, they could infuse it onto human genes to give them a feasible Trait.

I stared at the pages of nonsense notes, then the textbook I had been reading for the last few hours. The notes again. Textbook.

They wanted to combine immortality and fake Traits? No wonder they never succeeded.

I had to tell Inger now; I reached a dead end, and there was not much else I could do. The scientist's notes ended there, so I assumed they had never had time to test their theory.

At least the Preserv I was working on was coming along well. The solutions I made were not corrosive to the skin anymore, but I was still too afraid to test it on myself. Ideally, it would be absorbed by the body and flow throughout the bloodstream, increasing the longevity of those cells, delaying degradation, and spreading throughout the body. That was what I hoped, at least.

I walked out of the lab, dreading the cold again. Even if I stopped for a jacket, it would be pointless. Inger was not patient, and as quickly as I ran inside Etiquette, I would be in the snow again.

Back at Etiquette, the account checking lines were dwindling. Inger was not doing the work herself, and instead Lady Arabella and Miss Jessica were stuck waiting at the tables, looking bored out of their minds. Inger watched from the side, sipping from a wine glass and plastering a faux smile on her face whenever someone looked over.

"Inger, I finally figured out what the scientist was studying."

She barely looked my way. "Matilda, you already look like Pigladen trash again."

"Sorry." I had never minded my looks, and as soon as I'd sat down in the lab, being concerned about my appearance became secondary. "But anyway, they were trying to graft Traits onto a regular person. At least, they wanted to."

Inger's fingers tightened around the stem of her glass. "And how did they intend to do that?"

"By taking a Trait gene from a gifted person and transferring it to someone else." I guess I had to spell it out for her. It always seemed as though Inger did not have the patience to sit down and think things through but was always stumbling into the perfect solution.

"Go finish it then."

"I can't, Inger. No one in this region has a Trait."

Inger sighed deeply, the glass almost falling out of her hands. "Open the left cabinet under the sink and take out the box. Inside it, disguised as a pen, is the sample you will need."

My eyes widened. "Where did you get a Trait sample?"

"Where did you learn to be nosy? Go do as I said, and then tell me the results." She waved her hand, and I scurried away, my old questions now replaced with new ones.

I was panting by the time I reached my lab again, sweating even though I was freezing.

The questions I had about Inger outweighed the answers she gave me. This time, I could not even begin to understand why she had kept such a sample from me, or why, if she knew that much about Traits already, she never brought it up to help me.

That's been under the sink for years. I've always walked past it, and the answer was right there.

I hurried over to the sink, opening the cabinet like she had instructed me to. Sure enough, there was a pen sitting inside a box, but when I pressed down on the plunger, a thin glass tube shot out, landing in my palm.

I went under the bright lights to study it. It was the size of a darning needle, the label on it microscopic and written by a dedicated hand. I held it under the microscope, not quite sure what was inside. All I could see was a pale pink solution.

The floor swayed, and a sick feeling settled in the pit of my stomach. The handwriting was very familiar, detailing a date from eight years ago. A date of birth.

Tissue Sample: Princess Isobel Lagarde. Test for Inheritance: Positive.

***

Luck

Classes began later that day. Never in my entire life had I felt so alone.

A class of about twenty girls were already standing at their desks when I walked into the classroom with my school bag over my shoulder and my crinkled schedule paper in my hands.

"Hey, this is History Three, right?" I asked the nearest student.

"Yeah. Are you a new kid?" The girl wrinkled her nose, looking me up and down. "They must have messed up your schedule. Everyone here is sixteen and up, and you don't look a day over twelve."

I took a deep breath, flipping my hair over my shoulder and walking past her. "Actually, I'm fourteen.*" And skipped almost two whole levels of school to get here.*

I picked a standing desk in the back near the fireplace, laying my bag on it and taking out my notebooks. At least no one would stare at me if I was behind them, and the fire was warmest here.

I did have to stand on a few of my textbooks to write on the desk though, since they got taller toward the back.

There was too much on my mind. The tension between Papa and Mama. And there were these rumors going around town about Inger and her whole team, rumors that made me grateful I was not in front of the class in their line of sight.

Pizzette skipped in last, just as the bell rang. She took a desk near the window, ignoring the cold seeping through the glass and dropping her scruffy bag on the floor. She was wearing some guard's coat around her shoulders, and the uniform just did not look as flattering on her wiry frame.

The teacher sauntered into the classroom, her heels clicking in time like the hands of a clock. She stopped behind her desk, holding a thick tome and surveying us severely.

"I am Lady Arabella," she announced.

The class was dead silent.

"I will be teaching History Three this term. I know some of you were in History Two with me last term."

"Yeah. I was." The snotty girl who snapped at me raised her hand. "But there are some new people who just started here."

"That's how a school works, Liana. New people come and go."

"There's a fourteen-year-old in here. How did she get so ahead of everyone?" Liana crossed her arms, leaning back into her headrest.

Everyone turned and looked at me standing on books. A couple girls started laughing.

I stuck my chin up in the air. *Don't start crying, Luck. They're just jealous.*

"She's smart," Lady Arabella answered, looking straight at the back of Liana's head. "I remember another girl who graduated last year at fourteen. Wynona Dausen. She was quiet but studied hard. I think you should all challenge yourselves at some point in your life, or else you might become mediocre, like you Liana, someone old enough to get married."

The laughs were for Liana now, the attention no longer on me. I looked up at Lady Arabella, silently thanking her for saving me. I did not know how much longer I could have kept calm.

"Alright, settle down girls. We aren't a bunch of prepubescent boys."

Everyone quieted, pulling their elbows off the desks and standing up straight. The fireplace was roaring now.

"I think a fitting introduction to this term will be a brief discussion of the history of this country." Lady Arabella opened the book she was holding, her eyes skimming the pages. "I think history is useless when it is written down. You all know time travel used to be a free leisure, but not any longer. People used to record strings of history, events they knew were subject to change in a second. We really are spoiled if we live in a time where historians are so comfortable, they write it all down in these large textbooks. I propose we study history without the use of such lazy materials."

"Without a textbook?" Pizzette asked, making me groan. "How are we going to remember anything?"

"Because you live out history every day. No one forgot the Fourth World War, or the Third. And long before that, two others." Lady Arabella frowned, closing the book and dropping it on her desk. "Does anyone here really think about the past and what brought us all here?"

I shrugged, looking around and seeing everyone else doing the same.

Lady Arabella inhaled sharply, running a hand through her immaculate hair. "You privileged girls don't need to worry about anything. Here in Cyan, everything is perfect, right?"

"I wouldn't say that," a stout girl near the front said.

"You wouldn't say anything." Lady Arabella walked around to the front of her desk, the front row of students backing up a few inches. "Critically think about the war we left over four centuries ago, the war that began the new era. Can anyone tell me what happened?"

Liana raised her hand, going on with her answer before anyone even acknowledged her. "There was some intergalactic battle and a couple major countries collapsed. We didn't get this far in past years."

"That's a poor start. Someone should fix that."

"The organization that used to regulate scientific developments around the world finally gave in to the rebels," Pizzette said. "The war started because one experiment too many went wrong, and no one was controlling them."

"Control. You're right, the world was lacking order." Lady Arabella leaned against the desk, still as menacing as before. "Do you think we have peace now that the fighting is over, and we are all separated by borders and monarchies?"

"I think we have something close to it," the stout girl spoke again, standing on tiptoe.

"Do you like being so closed off from the world? There was a golden time when we used to like our neighbors."

"Well I don't want to intermix with mutants and start another race." Liana sniffed, turning her nose up. "That ended up in those freaks with Traits being born."

Lady Arabella's eyes darkened. "Do you know where Traits come from?"

"Not here." Liana blinked her long eyelashes, looking like an idiot. "And it should stay that way. The last time countries tried to partner with anyone, a whole war started and the Region was destroyed."

"But did some Traits cause the war?"

"I don't know." Liana looked down at her desk, finally conceding. "I guess that's why I'm here."

"Good." Lady Arabella smiled, walking up and down the rows while dropping some kind of leaflet on every desk. "This is why I love history. Even without interference, it loops over and over again. You can always learn from the past."

***

Pizzette

I was starting to get the feeling Lady Arabella had some personal grudge against time itself.

"How many of you know anything about the world from before the Fourth World War?" she asked, her voice still loud and commanding.

I raised my hand, forgetting that it would make everyone stare. "I know it was falling apart at the seams for a while. The destruction was so widespread that there are hardly any artifacts remaining from that time," I answered, wondering if she was starting to get annoyed with me.

"Yes, there was a growing sense of mistrust in the world, similar to now. Have any of you seen a relic from the old world?"

I held out the diamond around my neck, feeling the weight of it in my hands. "This was my father's. My mom once told me it was from Afrea, crafted hundreds of years ago."

Lady Arabella's eyes narrowed. "That's a royal diamond. Who is your father?"

Everyone turned around and stared at me, eyes bugging out of their heads. I was just as surprised as them. "Palmer Colfer, but he wasn't a prince or anything. I don't know where he got it."

Lady Arabella nodded, returning her attention to the leaflets she passed out. "Enough of that for now. Let's begin our first unit, the origin of the Lagarde line."

I scanned the paper, all the bullet points seemingly biased toward Madame Inger's agenda. There was a short description of her early life and the rest were stupid policies no one with a brain would support. Nothing on it was about the real Lagardes.

"There was a dark time following the end of the war where the countries separated and mended themselves. Years of pollution, famine, plagues, and fires had brought us to this point. Finally, when the world was almost in ruin, the rulers came to power. Some were descendants of royalty, or continuations of dynasties that had gone into hiding. The damage was the worst in Europia and across the ocean, and there was a need for order. The queen of Cyan, Idia Lagarde, returned with her family before the country was taken by anarchists. She was the first modern Lagarde as far as we're concerned. From then on, we have had strong generations of Lagardes. There was a time their family was very large, promising to continue the future, but tragedy always strikes. They say some autoimmune illness affected several generations in a row, leaving the most recent a small family of three: King Idrick, Queen Isobel, and Prince Indio Hayes. They were a symbol of hope to many, a sign that change might come to our stiff and proper society, but nothing ever goes smoothly in Cyan."

I shivered, resting my elbows on my desk. My legs were starting to ache, and her retelling was making the room spin. In Bark we did not talk much about Cyan, since their story was so unfortunate. Being here now was harrowing.

"Queen Isobel died in an accident during the prince's childhood. They say he never recovered fully from the loss, but he was a fine actor in my eyes.

"Prince Indio Hayes married Cyrana Kaleon eight years ago, a commoner the country fell in love with on sight. They had a daughter, Isobel Garnet Lagarde, a darling the whole of Europia adored. Less than two weeks after her birth, the palace caught fire, killing all of them. They say it was an electrical failure, some circuit improperly wired. We'll never know for sure, and the investigation ended years ago."

My knees buckled and I pitched forward, barely catching myself on the desk. No one looked back at me, probably too dazed to notice.

No wonder everyone here is so miserable.

"Madame Inger Kaleon, Cyrana's sister, took over Cyan from then on. She has yet to be crowned queen, but it will happen soon. The Kaleon dynasty will begin, continuing the success and beauty of this country while paying tribute to the last family we had."

"That sounds like a fairytale," Liana said wistfully. "A sad one."

"It's not a fairytale," Arabella snapped. "This really happened, and you were young, but you shouldn't be so callous now to call their suffering and sacrifice a fairytale."

"Sorry." Liana's face fell.

I stuck my hand up, breathing deeply. "Lady Arabella, what if people don't think Inger should be queen? I'm sure there's opposition from somewhere."

Her eyes flashed dangerously. "You shouldn't ask questions like that," she said in a strained voice. "Don't you understand? Inger's reign has already begun."

***

Mattie

I spent the rest of the day sitting in the lab, carefully following the directions in the notes and mixing the chemicals with the tissue samples from the pen. I started small at first, hoping I would not need so much to make the Trait substitute. Ten failed attempts later, then the mixture seemed to work. The structure I saw under the microscope matched the predictions in the notes.

This was as far as the notes could take me, unless I had missed something along the way. Still, I was on my own from now on.

I poured the substitute into a test tube, pulling the Preserv back into focus. If I dehydrated it, I might be able to compress it into a pill, but I was unsure of how to combine them. There were no details on that part of the procedure. At least I had better news for Lady Arabella when she walked into my lab later that day.

"What are you doing, roach?" she asked, walking around the side of my desk and picking up a vial. "This looks like sludge."

I stood up to grab it from her hands. "They're important tissue samples. Be careful."

"I can read, Matilda. Inger is waiting for this to be ready. I suggest you pull an all-nighter." She set the vial down, looking disgusted. "Artificial Traits. Imagine, that's the only way this useless country can amount to anything."

"Why not just let normal gifted people into Cyan?"

"You never took history classes, so I'll excuse that stupid comment. There is no law banning Traits from Cyan, but the rigid and judgmental society prevents a lot of forward movement. It always has." She picked at her manicured nails, above looking at me directly. "The new class I taught today proves that."

"Oh, you teach at Etiquette. I forgot."

"I'm so offended." Lady Arabella rolled her eyes. "We're all frivolous here. Inger is going to change that."

"I bet. How does Inger intend to do that anyway?"

Lady Arabella glared at the vial in my hands. "By showing the world what real power is, not whatever artificial hand the Lagardes and other families of Europia ruled with."

"But *how*? She...doesn't have much of a plan yet, right?"

Lady Arabella narrowed her eyes, frustrated. "You may have that fancy title, but her plans aren't yours to know until she decides to share. Inger is a secretive person."

"Are you sure she's not...stressed out? She has a lot going on at the same time—"

"Stop. Now. Why are you so concerned about Inger out of nowhere?"

I crossed my arms, shrugging. "She keeps secrets from me, and I feel like if I am to do my best work in this lab, she needs to let me in on the meetings. Let me figure out what all this is about."

Lady Arabella scoffed, shaking her head. "You? Making demands in this palace? Oh please." She turned on her heel, waving over her shoulder. "I expect that Preserv to be finished soon. Inger isn't the only person vying for immortality." She stopped in the doorway, shooting me one last glare. "Mind yourself. There's no crown on your head."

***

Luck

I was far too eager to return to my suite for the night with my dinner on a little tray. I left it on the desk and threw myself across the bed, shivering.

Everyone here was so cold. I had never felt so discouraged to even speak up in class. I hated it. Hated that I was going to be stuck here for years. My only motivation was an elevated title to carry me through my life.

I just wanted a moment alone. Too soon, fear started choking me, the familiar grip of anxiety closing around my throat.

He's coming back...

I sat up quickly, my head spinning. I had to stop thinking about what I missed.

I opened my French textbook, the words blurring together. *Oh no, this isn't working either.*

The tray of stewed chicken and vegetables was stinking up the whole room. I did not even feel like eating anymore. Habit had made me take it, along with a need to escape everyone's staring.

How did Wynona Dausen get through this place all by herself? No one was proud of me for being so successful. They were jealous, and it hurt.

Maybe I should write to Maude. She was probably having a worse time at Principles since it was so far away from us. She would appreciate a letter.

Not Mama or Papa. One for my sister.

I left my room with my tray, scurrying down the hallway without meeting anyone's eyes. Some of the girls had come with groups of friends already, and the rest seemed to fit right into existing cliques. Maybe I just needed to try harder.

The dining hall was set for dessert. A servant took my tray right out of my hands, offering me a little cone with mint chocolate chip ice cream in it. I shook my head, walking around them and over to the water pitchers. I would have sweets another day. I felt too sick already. Instead, I picked up a glass of water, the uniform ice cubes clinking together.

"Lady Lucienne Legrand, the baby."

I turned around quickly, some water sloshing out of my glass onto my hand. "Oh, hello Liana."

"You're not walking on books now?" One of the girls surrounding her, Greta or something like that, laughed.

"I just needed them to see. Excuse me." I tried to shuffle around Liana.

The wench stuck her leg out, tripping me so I fell into one of the dining tables.

"I think you still need them then." Liana's group giggled, closing around me like witches. "I bet you wish you had one to hit me with."

"Leave me alone." I stood up, massaging my elbow. The lace around it was torn. "You ruined my dress!"

"You're too young to wear such expensive clothes. Your father should return it to pay for the last two years of your elementary education."

Don't cry, Luck. They're just bullies. Don't let them get to you. "I'll be going."

"You think you're fooling us with your smart kid act, but we can see through it. Your father just paid off the staff here. That's how people like you ever make it far." Liana grabbed the edge of my sleeve, tearing the lace even more. "You rely on money and your pretty face. Your mother used to be dirt poor, and look at her pretending like your father."

"Don't talk about my parents." I slapped her hand away, crossing my arms and wishing the tables were not fencing me in with them.

"The Legrand family is a joke, and you know it. Get out of my high-class school." Liana flipped her hair over her shoulder and walked away, the rest of her crowd following. The girl on the end, Rena, tossed the rest of her ice cream at me. The cold slop landed in my nicely painted hair.

The whole dining hall was watching me, even the servants. No one said anything to me as I bent over and picked up my glass. Set it next to the pitcher carefully. Collected a pile of paper napkins and started walking back to my room.

Once I was out of their sight, I let the tears fall. *I guess that proves it. They are never going to like me here.*

I threw the dress on the floor, my heart racing so fast I could hardly catch my breath. It was happening again, that deep-rooted panic I always tried to bury coming to the surface and clutching my chest and covering my eyes and...

I ran to the bathroom, splashing cool water on my face, taking a few ragged breaths. I did not want to look in the mirror, not yet. Not anytime soon.

You're okay, Lucky. Just sit down and work on your letter. Just breathe. That's what Maude always told me. To *breathe.* As if I wasn't already trying.

I hunched over the counter, slowly controlling my hyperventilating. In. Out. Five seconds in between each measured breath.

There. Nothing's wrong. No need to panic now.

I turned on the faucet again, letting the water run over my shaking hands.

Christmas break could not come soon enough. I needed to get out of here tomorrow.

***

Pizzette

I told myself I was not hiding in my room, but that I was staying out of sight to remain undetected. *Because those are totally different things.*

A pile of books I borrowed from the biology classroom without permission were sitting on my desk. One of them focused on neuroanatomy, and with my mysterious memory blight taking forefront on my mind, I decided I might as well try and understand it. I had no intention to eat by myself in the dining hall, so I carried a tray back to my room and locked the door. Shut the windows. Kept the lights turned to their lowest setting so anyone who passed and examined the scant light emanating from under the door would think I was asleep and keep their pranks to themselves.

Since it was the top school in the country, I was a little surprised by how focused everyone was on being the prima popular girl instead of getting good grades. But what did I know, a little farmer girl from Bark?

The first book dove into the psychological connection to memory. Apparently, there were two parts of long-term memory:

procedural and declarative. I didn't recall ever having trouble talking or remembering how to read or write, so my procedural memory was intact. It was the other, made up of details and events, that was the damaged one.

I lifted a cup of hot cocoa to my mouth, taking a scalding sip. Someone had forgotten the sugar, unless that was how it was done here.

The book went on about the consolidation of memories and how it happened in different parts of the brain. Memories were supposed to strengthen over time between neural connections in the brain. The hippocampus was largely responsible for storing explicit memories, so by process of elimination, the problem was there.

What had that doctor done to me? Suddenly the cocoa did not seem so appetizing. Thinking about a stranger doing something to my brain to make it forget my past was frightening.

It was not fair that I never had a choice in the matter. What could be so horrible about my childhood that Mom wanted every memory of it removed?

I stood up, wondering how a late run to the palace would be received. Clint and the rest of the guards were polite about my escape earlier, but they had probably rotated to another part of the palace by now. Their replacements might not be so kind.

Still, I donned my cloak and boots and set out, heading for a different exit I had seen a few servants use. No one bothered me as I walked through the massive kitchens and right outside into the night. Cyans were good at minding their business, but they were almost a little too good at it. *Great to know no one would blink if I just walked into oblivion.*

The walk to the palace in the dark was intimidating. The building was huge, most of the rooms black and vacant. The few that had lights on were probably occupied by servants or Inger's team, all people I did not want to cross paths with right.

I walked into the palace kitchen still flanked by servants. One of them, a little girl who barely matched their heights, meandered inside holding a basket that was too big for her short arms.

"Let me carry that." I saved the basket before it fell, handing it to an older cook. "Come on. Give her something she can hold."

The cook gawked at me. "You talk?"

"I was trying to blend in." I turned back to the little girl, trying to smile reassuringly. "Don't let them bully you into carrying the heavier ones. Take it easy."

She stared at me with big brown eyes, all I could see under her hood. "Thank you."

"You're welcome." I darted through the palace kitchen knowing they would be less liberal here. I went through the familiar path to the library, hanging around in the hallway for a few minutes while the current occupants gathered their things. I peered through one of the clear glass panes, my heart stopping for a second.

Madame Inger and this man were standing in the library, sifting through a box of what looked like surveillance camera drives.

Did she know I snuck out? Was she going to punish me? I was not finding Etiquette one bit enjoyable, but I knew Mom paid for my tuition in full. Even though we had a chest full of diamonds at home, I did not like being wasteful.

"This is the one. I can't believe we missed it back then," Inger said, shoving the box back onto a low shelf. "Lock the library from now on. There might be copies of it in other bins."

"I can have Harry and Ida look for them," the man said.

"Those two kids are more unreliable than Codeware." Inger held the drives in her hands as she and the man walked toward the doors. I dove into the corner, pulling my cloak over my head like it would make me disappear.

"I'm beginning to wonder why we've left the doctor alone all these years. We don't need him anymore." The man's voice was getting closer.

"As a witness to the crimes that started our lives." Gosh, they were right in front of me.

"And Isobel?"

"Until the Preserv is finished. Those tissue samples might have been improperly stored. I wouldn't put it past the doctor."

"Arabella told me that Matilda is close to figuring it out. It's about time we let her in on all our secrets before…" Their voices faded away.

I stuffed a sleeve into my mouth to keep from crying out. *Isobel Lagarde? Were they talking about the missing princess?*

Lady Matilda was at Etiquette this morning. She helped me unlock my door. She was with them. Was she…evil? I could not think of a better word to describe the plot they were discussing. If my intuition was any good, Madame Inger was untrustworthy, a feeling I had right from the start.

It was possible that Princess Isobel Lagarde was alive, and that Inger was keeping it a secret. And the doctor. Everyone kept talking about a doctor I was yet to meet.

They were going to lock the library. I had to do my searching now or never. Maybe even find those drives Inger and that man were looking for.

I took one step out of hiding and right into someone's arms, and a gloved hand was pressed over my mouth, smothering my gasp. A sweet scent overtook my nostrils.

"Sorry, love, but you should not be here," a gentle voice whispered in my ear.

I need to find the doctor… I need to help the princess… I wanted to scream, but all the fight left me.

I felt my legs give out and did not stay conscious long enough to feel myself hit the ground.

***

Mattie

I woke up with my head flat on the lab table. It was late morning according to the clock on the wall. *I must have fallen asleep watching the experiment.*

I yawned, picking up the beaker and swirling it around. I thought I finally had it right. I had only used enough to cover for the body's cells, and by soaking the tissue sample for a few hours and allowing it to dissolve into the solution, the result was something I was sure would make Inger proud.

Of course, I could not test it on myself. Hopefully the first dose would not kill her.

I set the solution in a dehydrator to turn it into a powdery substance I could compact into pills. I was measuring how much to put inside one capsule when the door to my lab opened.

Lady Arabella stood by the doorway, frowning. With her almost transparent light hair and forlorn face, she looked to be in a trance. "We're having a meeting in Inger's office."

I stood up, confused. "Am I supposed to be a part of it?"

"Obviously. That's why I came to get you."

I hurried over. To my surprise, Lady Arabella handed me a small tart wrapped in a napkin. *Breakfast?*

Inger's office was stuffed with her advisors and partners in crime. The ever-boring, ever-quivering Daniels were seated across from each other. Miss Jessica, a rail-thin, black-haired menace and teacher at Etiquette, was next to Mr. Daniels, scraping the blades of two knives together. Lady Arabella took her place on Inger's right. To Inger's left was Norm, a behemoth of a man with jet black hair, unforgiving eyes, and huge fists that could have strangled countless people. There were three chairs left to choose from.

"Pick any," Inger said with a wave of her hand. "Harry and Ida are busy today. They're leaving soon."

I chose the one at the end of the table, so I did not have to touch elbows with a sadist or criminal. I nibbled on the tart and tried not to look at any of them too closely.

"The meeting has started," Inger yelled, making me jump. She had somehow rigged the walls, so they formed a soundproof barrier, the bluish light swathing them once she snapped her fingers. "Today, we shall be discussing my coronation in January, and the mess left over from the Burning."

I gulped, the tart sour now. She meant Isobel. *The poor girl is going to end up dead, right?*

"Isobel blends in well with the staff, so I'm keeping her around a little longer. She also remembers none of the events of the past few days. If the doctor complies, we might run a few tests on her." Inger took a sip of her coffee, grimacing and passing the rest to Arabella.

"We ought to get her out of the open," Miss Jessica snorted, the knives clinking. "One of these nosy students is going to recognize her despite the little costume she's wearing. Thanks to Mattie, they all know her face too well."

I blushed. "I only processed the pictures to have a basis for research. I didn't know they would become so popular."

"It's fine," Inger cut in. "Those girls are too flippant to look twice at a short kitchen aid in a hood. Isobel is the last living Lagarde, and after Cadmire's experiment, I want to see if she's worth anything to me."

"She doesn't mean that nicely," Lady Arabella clarified for me, taking a swig of the coffee and passing it to Norm. "This is too bitter."

"So, I'll enjoy it?"

"It suits your sparkling personality."

"Both of you, focus," Inger said, pulling a computer out from under the desk. She slid in a surveillance recording drive, pressing a few buttons to find the file she was looking for. "Who rescued my niece the day of the Burning?"

Surveillance footage. "I thought those were destroyed," I said, shoving the rest of the tart into my mouth.

"I knew it was futile to try and destroy all records. I believe there are several copies of this film, since the team that cleaned up the wreckage duplicated most of it in case an investigation ever called for it. We were lucky the chief investigator settled for half a million cizotes in our favor, but prying eyes might find the extras. Anyway, there are always things I can't control. I've shut down the entire library to find those tapes. Every single one of them."

She said it like a promise. I shivered, rubbing my arms to warm up. Sitting here with her team was not making me feel any more important. It was all a lie, and I let myself get swept up in it. *You don't have any other options, Mattie. There was nowhere else for you to go.*

"So here it is. Footage from the prince's wing and the princess's balcony." We all crowded around the computer screen to watch. Mr. Daniels ended up brushing against me. I shivered again.

"Just after eleven o'clock," Inger said in a low voice. "Eight years ago. I'd just set the throne room on fire, and Norm was killing the king."

The way she said *killing* shocked me, but the lack of reaction from everyone around me was a thousand times scarier. I had always known these people were dangerous, but to see their disregard for human life up close…I did not want to be one of them.

I would never let myself become that treacherous.

"I was inside my sister's suite, telling her and her husband today would be their last." Inger selected a specific video file, and suddenly we were inside their chamber, watching from above.

My stomach churned at the sight of a slightly younger Inger dressed all in black, blocking the doorway and holding a knife toward her sister and brother-in-law. They were huddled on the floor, arms tangled around each other, terrified.

No one had ever lied about Cyrana being the beauty Cyan had never seen. Her hair, like Inger's, was wavy, but hers was different shades of gold and brown mixed together. Her skin was a warmer tone, complimenting her wide-set dark brown eyes. There was something innocent about her image on the screen, as though she was a new fawn still getting used to the world around her. In a way, she was.

Cyrana died before she was nineteen years old.

"Today, it ends," I watched Inger say in a loud voice, brandishing her knife.

Prince Indio stood up, trying to reason with her. "Inger, please. Forget it all. This is ridiculous."

Inger ran the length of the room, knocking Indio back with her elbow and pressing the blade against his throat. "You love me. Say it. No more of this joking."

"He loves me, not you," Cyrana said, a tear sliding down her cheek. "He picked *me* over you."

Inger leaned forward on her elbows, bringing her face closer to the screen.

Cyrana raised her hands as if they held a mystical power, a dark look coming over her face. "Don't make me do this."

"Do what? You couldn't kill me if you tried. You've always been too weak, little sister." Inger cackled, still holding Indio captive. The prince was confused, his eyes darting between the two sisters.

"Cyrana, what is Inger talking about?" Instead of clarifying, Inger's blade barely bit into his skin, drawing a thin line of blood.

Cyrana flicked her hands upward and Inger suddenly pitched backwards. She regained her balance easily. "Is that all you have in you?"

Cyrana looked flushed, her body quivering. "I…I could do better."

Indio's voice cracked. "Cyrana, what just happened?"

We all heard the alarms begin as though they were right outside the door.

Indio's eyes flickered back to Inger. "What did you do?"

Inger's eyes were blazing. "If only you picked me to be your queen. It's a trick. She's tricking you."

"I don't believe it." Indio's eyes were full of concern only for Cyrana. "I don't love you, Inger. I'm sorry." He wrestled out of her arms, reaching for Cyrana.

"She's not even human," Inger muttered.

Cyrana stiffened, covering her face with her hands. Indio drew her close, still moving toward the door. "Inger, I've had enough of your insanity. We used to be friends, but I never knew you were like this, threatening your own sister."

"Can't you see that I'm better for you?" Inger shrieked, slicing the air with her knife. "I deserve everything Cyrana stole from me, and that includes your throne. You don't know what they did to me my entire life." She crossed the room, bent on attacking him.

Indio was about to open the door and shove Cyrana into the hallway when the knife entered his chest.

Cyrana screeched, tackling Inger to the ground.

Indio staggered backward, and then fell against the wall, clutching his chest.

Vomit came up my throat. I was going to be sick, but I could not tear my eyes away.

Cyrana punched Inger in the face twice, shoving her to the side, and then scrambled over to Indio's dying body. She knelt next to him, whispering words to him no one in the room could hear.

Then he was dead, and Cyrana was alone with Inger.

"Inger, stop. We'll never make this right. I'm sorry about what happened to us here all these years." Cyrana sat up, her face distraught. "You will always have another chance."

Inger towered over her, backing her against the wall. Cyrana whimpered.

"Not at Cyan. Not at the crown. Unless my sister and niece are also dead, I will never fulfil my purpose for being created."

I flinched as Inger grabbed her sister's throat and-

The Inger next to me was calm as she watched herself commit the murder, not the slightest bit of emotion coming across her face.

Then she clicked a button and cleared away the footage before we could see how she had reacted.

"This is it," Inger whispered, switching to a different angle. "I left and went into hiding after this. I figured the smoke was enough to take care of Isobel."

I saw the royal nursery through the shaded view. My heart hammered, horrible sadness washing over me. Even through the tape, you could hear the quiet snoring from the little room. The baby was asleep, oblivious of her parents' murders down the hall.

Then the figure appeared. He snuck into the room just as smoke began to pour into the halls. Thick and black, promising only flames and destruction.

Inger zoomed in on his profile, trying to see their face. He exited the room with Isobel in his arms. He ran swiftly down the hall and through the double doors leading out onto the balcony.

For a moment, he stood there holding Isobel while she cried. Then he whispered a prayer, kissed Isobel's forehead, and dropped her over the rails.

He heaved a sigh of relief. Someone must have been waiting to catch her. It was only when he turned around that we got a clear view of his face.

Just for an instant, then he ran back inside, maybe to help the others.

Little did he know that it was too late. The rest of the Lagardes were already dead.

The tape suddenly froze. I looked to Inger whose face had gone pale.

"I know that necklace," she whispered.

I looked back and recognized it as well. I had seen it around a student's neck just yesterday.

Oh, how it all began.

***

Pizzette

I woke up in my Etiquette suite, tucked into bed like nothing had transpired the night before. When I rolled over, the clock on the wall read fifteen minutes past ten in the morning. I had overslept, which was a normal occurrence.

My memory was less than perfect, but I had not imagined the conversation between Inger and that man in the library. I did not make up the stranger drugging me in the hallway.

Yet here I was, and there was no one sitting around to explain why. No servant was waiting outside to yell at me for being late. No one had brought me breakfast.

Everything continued as normal, which just did not make any sense.

I sat up slowly, looking at all the corners of my room for cameras. Was this a test? Did Madame Inger have a team of detectives studying me? Did she think I was a spy? I could only assume that the stranger who grabbed me was one of her loyal guards, so I had no reason to believe I was safe.

I stepped into the bathroom for some privacy, hoping her spies were not that voyeuristic. I splashed cold water on my face, pinching my cheeks to bring some feeling back into my body. I went numb when I was terrified, and right now my body was freezing over.

Since I was already late to class, I took my time bathing and dressing. In an effort to blend in, I put on one of my nicer gowns and brushed out my hair, braiding it back in a Cyan braid, tying the tail with blue ribbons. I forced on earrings and bangle bracelets, trying to make the most of my time. I even put on my nice white boots, tying the laces into fancy knots I had learned from a friend at the docks. I put my father's diamond back on after a moment of hesitation, touching it for comfort. *Don't incriminate yourself. Maybe you really did have a dream about last night.*

I passed a few servants on my way to French class, their nonchalance calming me. There were no guards waiting around the corner to arrest me, so I simply skittered across the school.

Miss Jessica barely looked at me when I came into the classroom late. I had missed picking a decent seat, so I was stuck in the back by the fireplace that instantly made me sweat.

"What are we doing?" I asked the girl in front of me as I dropped my bag on the floor.

"Writing an essay about our hopes for the future in French. She wants to see how much we already know." The girl turned back around. I got a glimpse of her three pages of writing and swooned.

Besides a few insults and general phrases, I did not know much else. I took out my notebook and tried to pretend, the measly exercise doing little to distract me. My mind started wandering.

Isobel Lagarde might be in danger, and you're just standing here. Can't you do something?

I glanced up at the windows. It was snowing outside, the wind blowing it all around the place. I could slip out again, but in broad daylight a girl from Etiquette would stand out too much. If only I had someone who could get me inside. *Maybe your stranger in the hallway. The friend who drugged you and maybe carried you back to Etiquette in the dark. I'm sure you'll find them around here.*

Maybe if it got blistery enough, I could go running. *Yup. No one would see you then.*

French ended, leaving me with no ideas and a blank essay. I turned it in with the others, filing out before Miss Jessica could start yelling at me. She did not seem like she had the temper to deal with any inconvenience lightly, so I strove to stay clear of her anger.

Everyone went down to lunch. I lingered at the back, unsure of where to go or who to talk to. In Bark, you could tell the person who delivered mail your troubles. In Cyan, it was no one's obligation to care if you had someone to sit with at meals or talk to. Half of the people here were suck-ups to Inger, so they were eliminated as options. Everyone else was on varying levels of being disagreeable.

Starving, I filled my tray with small plates of everything, carrying it back to my room. I left it on my bed and opened the windows, hoping the light would inspire me. The shutters flipped over, disturbing a little piece of paper that must have been balanced on the edge. I picked it up, the handwritten message completely foreign to me.

Pizzette, don't be an idiot and go back to the library with Inger swarming it. If you are looking for the doctor, you should go to his old office. The guy used to work at the palace.

What the heck? I was certain I was being watched. There had to be someone waiting.

But no one came inside yelling. Steam just rose from my tray, slow and wafting like the snow outside.

Only Clint knew I had been looking for the doctor. Was he helping me?

There was only one way to find out. I shoveled down my lunch, slipping on one of my light-colored cloaks and hiding my hair in a hat.

If I had a guard on my side, maybe Inger would not be such a threat.

***

The servants in the kitchen did not particularly like me, so I made no attempt to blend in as I walked toward the palace with them. I pitied the unlucky crew that, after cooking meals here, had to walk to the palace to work while the rest took breaks or cleaned indoors. Last night had been cold enough, but today's wind was unbearable. I ran ahead, my boots leaving deep prints in the snow.

I had to find Clint. All I remembered were his amber eyes and a dry sense of humor. I left the kitchen with a pile of towels in hand as a meager disguise and wandered the halls. Every guard wore the same black armor and uniform with the blue accents and countless weapons hanging off them. The ones outdoors had their coats, but that was not enough to distinguish them once they came inside.

Coats. I still have Clint's coat. I had to go back for it. Maybe we could trade information.

"You're in the wrong hallway, window cleaner," someone barked behind me. I whirled around, my heart stopping when I recognized the man from last night.

"Oh, sorry. Thanks for telling me." I tried to sidle around him, keeping my head low. I clearly did not look like a servant up close.

Without a word, he reached out and grabbed my arm. The towels fell to the floor.

"Merci?" Maybe French would help my case.

"Who are you?" he asked, his tight hold on my wrist painful. "Who let you into the palace?"

"I'm just a window cleaner like you said…it's my first day." I fought the tremor in my voice. *Don't give yourself up. He knows nothing until you tell him.*

"Bullshit." He studied my face, his eyes flickering over my body curiously. My cheeks reddened, but I stood still, wishing I could pull my hat down to cover my entire body and disappear. "What's that?" He gestured to my necklace.

Ugh. No servant would have a diamond around their neck, genius.

"Family heirloom?"

"I don't believe it." He seized my other arm, pulling me down the hall. "I don't believe a word you just told me."

"Wait." I tried not to scream. *There's no need to…oh screw it.* "Where are you taking me?"

"You'll find out."

"*Norman Chester,*" a voice called down the hallway. Miraculously, the man stopped, swiveling around to see who had interrupted him.

It was another guard. *Thank goodness.*

"I don't have time for this." Norman sounded resolute. The guard stopped in his tracks, nervous in front of him for some reason. "What?"

"I...the girl...You see she came here not long ago. My group escorted her back to Etiquette."

"Try to explain yourself again, Tomas. Maybe this time you'll get it right."

"Clint said she seemed bored. I think she just likes to wander." Tomas had a docile face, like he did not know how to lie. That made his little explanation more believable.

"Yeah, school is boring," I added.

Norman completely ignored me. "Really? A wanderer?"

"Yes. I'll take her back." Tomas's hands knit together. He was starting to crack.

Norman looked at me, and then at Tomas again. "What's your name, girl?"

"Pizzette Marie-Rose Colfer."

"Fine. I'll tell the staff to watch after this one. Tomas, take her back to Etiquette and tell your pathetic group to do their job. If teenage girls can sneak into the palace, there isn't much hope for the future of this country." He let me go, practically shoving me into Tomas.

"Yes, sir." Tomas took my hand gingerly, pulling me away from Norman as quickly as he could. "It won't happen again."

"Thanks," I said once we put some distance between us and Norman. "I'm sorry for getting you in trouble." I had not seen Tomas with Clint's group, but they had all been wearing jackets and hoods. My short-term memory was not reliable either. I was used to missing details about every situation no matter how focused I thought I was.

"That's fine. I don't like to see them berating the servants." We walked down a wide staircase, passing windows completely blacked out with paint. "I guess you're not one of them anyway."

"Yeah. I thought I could find some more information on someone here, but I ran into that guy. Who is he anyway?"

"Norman J. Chester, Madame Inger's oldest friend." We entered a long hallway, identical to most of the others. This path was longer than the one I had come through, and more exposed, but no one approached us. I guess the snakes stayed in the dark upper floors.

"Oh. I didn't know…" *What? Inger has friends?* "Never mind."

"You're a strangely curious girl. What is it about the doctor you're so bent on finding?"

"Well, Dr. Cadmire just…" *Erased my memory. The usual.*

One of the doors opened. Lady Matilda walked out, but she was nearly unrecognizable in a shabby dress with her hair in two messy braids. I did not think the title even matched anymore. She looked at Tomas with a passing glance, but I felt him instantly tense. Her eyes lingered on me a second longer, the corners of her mouth twisting.

"Do you know where Inger is?" she asked Tomas. "I have to tell her something."

"I'm assuming the dining room."

Lady Matilda nodded. "I'll check there."

Tomas was quiet for a few minutes. When the silence became heavy, I tried to continue my explanation. "He knew my mother. I just want to ask him some questions."

"He's hardly at the palace these days, but his office is still here. Do you want me to show you?"

"Yeah, but I think you would be executed right after." I stopped in front of a wide window, pressing my hand against the cool glass. Restraints. From now on I would have people watching me. Inger would know I was a problem to monitor. "I can't do that to someone I just met, especially when they helped me."

Tomas walked up behind me. I could see his reflection in the ghostly white outside, tall and broad-shouldered, a contrast to his gentle voice and timid nature. "You forgot Clint's jacket. He's been grumbling about that whenever he goes outside."

I had one last pass into the palace. "Thank you so much. I guess I'll bring it tonight."

"Be careful, Lady. The palace is a nightmare in the dark." He lowered his voice, his hand landing next to mine on the glass. "I see flames until dawn, as though the fire never stopped."

***

Luck

I stood in history class waiting for Lady Arabella to show up, with my head tucked in a book so no one would bother me. Liana and her crew had expanded. It was clear most of the class was part of her posse now.

I would never understand what I did to be hated by so many. Maybe it was my title or my family's name. *But those things don't define me. I'm not just a couple of adjectives. I'm a human with a life worth something.*

The words on the pages turned blurry. *I'm not good at applying that to others though. Maybe I deserve their insults.*

Lady Arabella came into the classroom holding a mug of coffee, her face looking bored. "Don't ask me why I'm late. Take out your notebooks. We're going over the Fourth World War's effects on the environment today."

After one and half grueling hours of writing out the terms of the Environment Restoration Act, I walked to the dining hall to collect my dinner. I waited until Liana's gang passed before picking up the scarce remainders and starting towards my room. I realized halfway there that I forgot to grab a drink. *Luck, just this once can you pull yourself together and focus?* I turned around, cursing myself.

The dining hall had some guests. Lady Arabella must have stayed after class to make an announcement. She was accompanied by two of Inger's team members whose generic names had slipped my memory. I did not want to be rude and disrupt their speech, so I leaned against the wall, balanced the tray on my fingertips, and waited for it to be over.

"First and foremost, we wish to make you all aware of a security adjustment," Lady Arabella said, sounding like she was reading from a card. "We know you are all silly young girls with eyes for the palace and nobles' sons, but you are not permitted to leave this building unless given permission by the staff. And you are certainly not allowed to use the kitchen staff to sneak into the palace."

It was dead silent. I looked around for a red, apologetic face. Was someone really stupid enough to get caught sneaking out?

"The trip to the Sea of Cyan in a few days will continue as planned. Just know that any future infractions will result in punishment more severe than just expulsion." She smiled sweetly, but her eyes betrayed her. "I wouldn't want to see one of you missing one day."

"From class because you got kicked out," the stout woman next to her coughed. "Not any other reason."

"Yes." Lady Arabella waved like a mock princess, and then sauntered toward the exit, surrounded by her guards and the odd couple.

It took a few minutes for the chatter to resume. As I filled a glass of water, someone tapped my shoulder.

"Was it you, Lucienne?" Penny Brutus, a girl who had to pull up a chair every day to sit mostly behind everyone at Liana's table, asked me. "Were you sneaking out?"

"No."

"You never eat in the dining hall. We all thought it was because you were going somewhere." She smiled devilishly. "It was actually because you had no friends."

I did not ask her to leave me alone. I did not try to skirt around her and run to my room crying.

Instead, I picked up my glass of water and splashed it on her stupid-looking face.

"Oops." I set the glass down next to the pitcher, considering throwing my dinner at her for good measure. "I think I spilled a little on you."

I heard Liana's high laughter from across the hall. I did not acknowledge her friends as I walked out, pretending Penny was not whining and that everyone was staring.

I nearly ran into a servant who was carrying a stack of plates too high for her to see around. "Hey!" I whirled around, trying to be patient. "You almost ruined my...Oh, you can barely see." The servant was the youngest I had ever seen, covered up so I could only see part of her face and her rough hands.

I did not miss a little smirk on her face.

"I saw you throw your water at that girl," she said in a delicate voice, giggling. "It was funny."

I could not help but smile. There was something infectious about this girl's easy laugh. "She was bullying me. Sometimes, you have to pour water on the witches."

She giggled again. "Thank you for making me laugh. I've been so upset recently."

Poor thing. She's probably some lost orphan who needs a place to stay. "I'm sorry, little girl. I hope you feel better."

"I will." She tried to put on a brave face, I assumed. "After I find Marmi, everything will be okay."

Her optimism made my eyes burn. *Did she lose her mother or something? I doubt she's just going to float back into her life.*

"I hope so. Goodnight...?"

"Petrakova." She held out her hand, the stack of dishes teetering. "Petrakova Selle."

"Right." I shook her hand. She was so polite for a little girl. Her mother, Marmi, had done a better job raising her than the parents of Cyan's best and brightest. "I'm Lady Lucienne, but my friends call me Luck." *I mean, if I ever had a friend, that's what they would call me.*

"Okay, Luck." She beamed, and then walked away quickly.

The moment was over. She looked at me like I was someone special, like I was her hero. Maybe that was just how all little kids were, so very trusting of people older than them, so confident that they would never want to hurt them.

Wait until you see the real world, Petrakova. Once you get to my age, you're no one's darling.

***

Mattie

There was no reason for Inger to be taking an entire school of ladies to the Sea of Cyan in the middle of the winter less than one month before her coronation.

Yet she was doing it anyway. Lady Arabella said it was to calm her nerves. I thought she was just irrational. But what was I, the girl about to finish the first batch of Preserv spiked with a potential false Trait? A genius?

Inger came into my lab just after nine in the morning, breathless from running, an activity she never considered when walking was an option. "Is the Preserv finished?"

"Somewhat. I'm just checking the measurements to make sure it won't be too much."

Inger reached into the pocket of her pantsuit, distracted. She was not even listening to me.

"The pills might be too massive, so I want to run the math again."

Inger was busy dumping blood red pills into her palm from a container, counting them religiously. Without a warning, she picked up several of the Preserv capsules and swallowed them dry.

I was beginning to think I hated Inger, but some part of me did not want to watch her die.

I punched her in the stomach, my fist barely interrupting her. "You're going to be sick if you take too many."

"Matilda, I'll be fine."

"And what are those other pills?" I felt blood rushing in my ears looking at the woman who had murdered her family for selfish reasons. Lied to secure herself to the throne eventually. Hid her niece to have a test subject within arm's reach at all times.

"They make me feel stronger." Inger picked up most of the other Preserv capsules, filling a small plastic bag with them. She did not even bother to label it. "Nothing will kill me."

"Fine." My mind filled with too many thoughts, the ever-present headache at the center of my brain growing worse.

I had to find Isobel and set her free. Whatever she had been given after the kidnapping had nullified her memory. I had to convince Inger she was dead or something, and then I would take the tapes and get Inger arrested…No. All the guards and all the officers only answered to one leader. No matter how dire my case sounded, they would never listen to the lowlife girl without a family, wealth, or article to call her own. No. They were too cowardly to turn their backs on Inger.

They were all too afraid.

"Mattie." Inger's voice brought me back to reality. "Make more of these. I need more." She studied my face, the corner of her mouth lifting. "What are you thinking?"

"Nothing." I lowered my head, fuming. *Always nothing.*

"Good." She slammed the lab door shut, leaving me shivering and alone.

She had taken them after a quick glance. She did it so casually, measuring out the dosages before I even had a moment to correct her and pairing them with those blood red pills.

It was almost like she already knew what the Preserv was supposed to look like. As if she did not really need me this entire time.

I leaned on the countertop, my eyes burning.

What is wrong with me? Why can't I just be…Useful? Do the right thing?

Maybe I was no better than I wanted myself to be.

***

Pizzette

Despite Lady Arabella's warning, I knew I had to leave again. This time, since I knew there would be eyes on the kitchen exit, I put on Clint's coat and walked out in plain sight.

I hoped my simple black pants and shoes would do enough to make me blend in with the other guards touring Etiquette. I had tied my hair up and covered it with Clint's hood, praying no one would stop and talk to me when I walked out the main entrance.

No such luck.

"Where are you going?" I did not recognize the gruff voice. I had a feeling this guard was not the type to call me *lady* and offer me a coat.

"The palace. Sir."

"Who are you? I was not aware that one of the guards on this rotation was instructed to leave."

"My name is…" I stalled, the lie as false as my uniform. I clasped my hands behind my back, shivering. "Never mind. Listen, I've got places to be right now."

The man stepped forward off the stairs, two of the lower guards watching with wide eyes as he pulled the hood off. My long hair tumbled over my shoulders.

Surprise.

"She's one of the students," he sputtered, the sight of my hair apparently shocking. *I thought the voice did me in. I guess I was wrong.*

"Yeah. Could you let this one slide?"

"I'm taking you to Madame Inger. She'll deal with you swiftly."

No. Without thinking, I kicked him in the shin and started sprinting toward the palace like an idiot. I tripped over a pile of hardened snow, my face scraping against a patch of ice.

The guard was immediately on top of me, wrestling my arms behind my back. "Hold still, rascal. Are you one of the ones here on scholarship?"

"No," I spat, still wriggling. "I paid tuition in full." *Did I?*

"Too bad. It was a waste of money." He hefted me off the ground, dragging me by my hair toward the palace. Inger.

"You know Inger is going to hurt me. You know I won't just be kicked out."

The guard did not say anything. Fear started to claw at my insides, making me swoon.

"Please. I'm just a kid. Kids make mistakes."

"Cyan has enough kids. We won't miss one."

His words were a punch in the gut. And then his fist followed, knocking the wind out of me. I doubled over, gasping.

"Stand up straight or I'll hit you again."

I dared him. "I thought guards were supposed to protect people."

"I'm not losing my job over a stupid girl like you. Now stand up." I refused, and he punched the side of my face.

It hurt to keep the defiant act going. "You're about to get sued by a very rich family."

"I'll see to it Madame Inger kills you all."

I tripped again, expecting the blows to come. *What did he just say? Are these people sadistic?* He was leading me to my death, if it was not meant to happen right here.

"Wait. Hear me out." I scurried back on all fours, the snow snaking up my sleeves. "What are you doing?"

Out of nowhere, I heard someone running across the courtyard. "Bonne! Bonne, what are you doing?"

Oh, thank goodness. Clint, my helper from the inside, had finally come to help me.

Bonne excused himself bluntly. "She's the sneak. It's time she faces punishment."

"So, you beat on her yourself?" Clint picked me up like I weighed nothing, holding me against him possessively. "She's a student, a kid, and a *girl*."

Bonne snarled. "You know that means nothing to Inger."

"That should mean something to you, and you could get all of us fired for misconduct. We follow Inger's orders, not make up our own." I could not see Clint's face behind me, but I could hear his heart in my ear. He was terrified. Stepping out of line did not warrant a happy ending for either of us.

"Inger would have Norman Chester do the beating anyway. I was just making it easier for him."

"Get out of my sight, Bonne. And don't speak a word about this to anyone. Are you the one responsible for the bruises on those seamstresses? Have you been delivering punishments on your own agenda around here?"

Bonne's smug face fell. "Clint, you aren't looking so loyal to the crown right now."

"I am loyal to the crown," he said resolutely.

"Then give me the girl and go back to work. She's breaking the rules."

"Because of me." Clint picked up the material around my shoulders. "I lent her my coat and she was bringing it back. She's not the girl Inger's after. She was just being nice."

Bonne held Clint's gaze for a few tense seconds, then shook his head. "Fine. Don't mention this to anyone, or I'll turn you in as well."

"We'll see how that works for you."

We watched him leave, and then I turned around and hugged Clint, my sanity gone. "Thank you so much. He was about to—"

"Crazy girl," Clint sighed, lightly touching the side of my face. "Come inside. You face is cut."

"Really?" *Battle scars. I've always wanted those.* "You don't have to worry about that. I just need to go to Dr. Cadmire's office."

Clint stopped in the arched entryway; his back suddenly rigid. "What is your obsession with danger, lady?"

"I don't have an obsession. Just questions with answers that require some digging." I winced, my stomach throbbing in pain. "Wow, he can really punch."

"All of us guards are trained to kill. It was probably ingrained in his body to hit you as though you were an armed rebel." Clint led me through the dark halls, our destination only known to him.

"I am a rebel. I've always been." I glanced at him, wondering why he was not bringing up the note or the doctor. "That's why I was hiding in that hallway last night."

He looked down at me, confused. "I have no idea what you are talking about, lady."

My blood chilled. "Wait... Do you even know my name?"

"You never told me, and I'm not the type to look it up." He opened the door to a dusty little office and motioned for me to walk inside. His eyes scanned the corridor for passing guards.

"Wait." *The letter. Whoever left me the note already knew my name.* "You really don't?"

"Yes. Now go inside before we both get caught." I did, but instead of feeling reassured, I felt like I was walking into the last chapter of my life.

"It's Pizzette, by the way."

"Really? Not very common around here." Clint frowned, looking down at me. "What does it mean?"

"I don't really remember." I pursed my lips, feeling more ridiculous by the second. I decided to change the topic before he dwelled on my confusion any longer. "Is this the doctor's office by any chance?" I asked, still clinging to a little hope.

"No, but someone left a few of his books here." He shut the door and flipped on the lights. It was a small room with a table and two chairs. A shelf filled with medical supplies. "They use this room as an infirmary of sorts. Sit down and I'll patch you up."

"Are guards also trained to revive?" I mumbled, pinching my palms to stay focused. My mind was racing.

"If we're injured in conflict it makes us less useless." Clint opened up a package of antibacterial wipes, shaking one out. "But this is basic first aid."

"What kind of conflict have you been in?" I asked, bracing myself for the sting on my cheek.

Clint was quiet for a moment, his hand on the side of my face, the only thing I was aware of. That, and the heat under my skin. *Idiot. You put so much blind faith in the bogus idea that he was your secret savior.*

"Plenty of minor ones. The only severe one was..." He dropped the wipe in the trash basket, pulling out a tube of antibacterial ointment. "The Burning. It happened shortly after I began working here. I'd recently turned seventeen."

I was at a loss for words. "Clint..." *He was so young. How did he ever come back to this place, then? I can't imagine how haunting it must be.*

"There were many people I tried to save," he said quietly, smoothing a bandage over my cheek. "But I was not successful. I only came back to work to try and make it up to the people I failed."

There was hardly any emotion in his amber eyes. Instead, his jaw tightened, the tension the only indicator of his feelings. He was someone who tried to tamp it all down, pretending he was unaffected and unhurt. But in moments like right now, I could sense the war he was battling internally. The regret he clung onto.

"I guess that's why I've been trying to help you." He patted my cheek lightly, the bandage secure and comforting. "To make myself feel better."

"Thank you." He was not my secret stalker-savior-drug-friend, but he was someone I trusted. "I really appreciate your help."

He could not take his eyes off my face, as if he was looking at me for the first time. No, not me, but my diamond.

"That's…that's a pretty necklace you're wearing."

My hands closed around the diamond. "Thanks. It belonged to my father."

He stared at it a few seconds longer, and then pointed at the table. "The books. I'll give you fifteen minutes, and then we have to get out of here. I don't want anyone getting suspicious."

"Okay." He left the room, probably assuming I needed privacy to read. Or maybe he thought I was about to start crying.

I could not imagine why.

I picked up the first book, losing myself in Dr. Cadmire's sloppy handwriting and confusing entries. There were no clocks in the room, so I tried to skim the text for something important. Nothing caught my eye until I was halfway down the last two pages.

Memory Neutralizer; to be tested on request.

I took a deep breath and finished reading the page.

I do not know if this procedure will work. As always, I'm pioneering technology the world might be better off without. For the sake of my job and sanity, I should continue. After the failure of my last experiment, I need to lose myself in another project.

The brain generates electricity, obviously not the voltage powering the city. Every firing neuron generates an action potential. Our current theories state that memories are strengthened between neural connections and consolidated in the hippocampus. If I alter the electrical current between certain areas of the brain and essentially rewire the neurons comprising the memory-specific regions, I may have some success with erasing memories. It will work like a circuit box, feeding the wires in one end and disrupting memories. After the procedure, the damaged pathways should mend themselves, but recalling the old explicit memories should be nearly impossible. Misinterpreting certain emotions may be a side effect, as the emotional attachment to early memories is destroyed.

I would love to be my own subject and test this on myself, but someone has already put in a request. Someone always puts in a request for their downfall.

I dropped the notebook, suddenly near tears.

That was it? There was a piece of metal in my head changing the way my brain created and stored memories? Mom had stood by and let the doctor do that to me?

Who did I really have to trust, if my own mother let my memory to be taken from me?

Tears started rolling down my face, and I could not pull myself together to dry them.

I just want to go home. Let me out of here.

When I walked into the hallway crying, Clint was quick to throw an arm around my shoulder.

"I'm sorry. Loss is an immeasurable pain. I would not wish it upon anyone."

I was not sure what loss he was talking about, but I hugged him back, needing the solid reassurance that someone cared.

My own mother asked the strange palace doctor to try out his memory experiments on me and erased every memory I had of Cyan and my father. I did not even know how to miss him.

I was pretty out of it until I was back at Etiquette. Clint let me keep the coat, and even offered to walk me to my suite.

"I'm okay. I need to be by myself for a while."

"Alright. Goodnight."

I let myself into my room, walked into the bathroom and started running a hot bath. I wanted to sleep but felt too anxious to sit down. The heat would help.

I stared at my reflection in the mirror, my heart sinking when I could barely recognize myself.

Pizzette Marie-Rose Colfer hardly cried. When I did, it turned my whole face into a different version of myself. One that felt as bruised and damaged as she looked. My cheek was a little swollen under the bandages. There was a bruise blossoming over my stomach and rib cage.

No little scars on my head.

There was something undeniably wrong with Cyan. From the laissez-faire teachers to the way everyone acted like nothing was wrong. They all enjoyed their money and fancy balls without asking themselves who their own leader was. It was a nightmare within the palace, the center of the most glamorous court in the world. Where others saw beauty in privacy and coveted palace chandeliers and nobles, I saw treachery. Inger Kaleon and her team were bloodthirsty, and apparently so were most of their guards.

If Clint had not helped me, I would have been expelled or thrown into prison. The other two guards simply watched Bonne drag me through the snow. I wondered, if Clint never made an appearance, would they have stayed silent?

I saw that everywhere and was beginning to see it in myself as well. *Etiquette is full of bullies. The servants here bully each other, you bully yourself.* When would it end? Why was everyone so defensive?

I stepped into the bath, still cold and numb.

Isobel Lagarde's possible survival was like a fairy tale people chose not to believe. There were no conspiracy theories, or at least people questioning publicly what Inger said about her. At least in a healthy world there would be a little suspicion, a little mistrust so that you had time to get to know and appreciate someone.

In Cyan, I knew nothing about anyone else, and they knew nothing about me.

The problem was that most of them did not seem to think anything of it.

***

Part 4

Luck

We're all a forest of fallen trees.
Why didn't you stay along with me?
And last alone while the dawn dwindles to dusk.
We were always just the two of us in the brush.

Maude's rare singing voice filled my dreams. I missed being home more than ever, the past week at Etiquette more terrible than the first. The only reprieve from the constant attacks from Liana's crew was the coach ride down to the Sea of Cyan. I signed up for the coach that was practically empty, everyone on it just as miserable as I was.

No one talked to me, so I took a nap and tried to be excited. My new skates and coat, both custom-made by the palace seamstresses and shoemakers, were a delightful shade of blue with green accents. Picking out the colors and watching the servant's needle's fly was the most fun I had in a while. Being able to wear what they created right in front of me felt surreal. I knew clothes and accessories came from factories, but I had never imagined a factory's speed and precision could be replicated by a mere servant.

They said Princess Cyrana loved to go up there, spend hours enraptured with the sewing machines and bolts of fabric imported from all over the world. Next to the library, the Rotunda was her favorite part of her home.

Without her there…well, some things never went back to normal.

I wanted to ask one of them to teach me how to sew but had been too impish.

After this trip, I would have to start planning Christmas gifts. Maude and I used to run to the shops the weekend before Christmas, leaving with arms full of bags and mugs of hot chocolate. I wondered if she would still make time for me with her trip to Gallen happening at practically the same time.

At least I would have some peace. A break was all I needed now.

***

Pizzette

The trip took nearly two hours. I spent most of the time on a crowded bus sleeping.

My dreams were about metal boxes and scalpels that left no scars. Shadowy faces I probably used to know before they went out through one door and never came back.

I needed someone to be mad at, but the people here were too unfamiliar to reduce my anger. I wanted to yell and scream, hit someone.

Clint would tell me to calm down, stay out of trouble. I had not seen him since he saved me from Bonne, but I passed by Tomas several times during his rotations. He told me Inger was still angry about students sneaking out even after she upped security at all entrances to the palace. Servants had to wear tags or badges to be let in. My injury earned some questions from my teachers, but so far Inger was still in the dark.

That was fine. I never wanted to go back to that place again.

The buses stopped about ten miles from Pigladen. The Sea of Cyan stretched beyond us into the horizon, a glimmering blanket of blue. Everyone stalled getting off the buses, transfixed by the beauty of the light reflecting off the icy surface, the trees swaying in the gentle wind.

It began to snow as we laced up our boots on the frozen riverbank. Light glinted off the metal, landing on my bandaged cheek. It was silent, the absence of the leaves combined with the noise of cars and shouting gone. No coins dropping out of pockets or insults flying under the radar.

It was idyllic, completely serene.

Lady Arabella spoke nonsense about the economics behind maintaining the Sea while we began skating. I had never skated before, but I managed not to embarrass myself. Someone started singing, and eventually Lady Arabella stopped preaching and let us be.

Cyan seemed like it had the potential to be a pleasant place at times. With music in my ears, stark cold against my cheek, and the strain of exercise on my body, the salty little dictatorship of a country was exciting. For a few seconds, I did not mind being here because I would never have seen any of this in Bark. I tried to imagine my parents here, or at least Mom swirling around on the ice with a shadowy man. *Does she even know how to skate? Did he?*

I wondered what he used to do to make her smile. It seemed like all we did was argue with each other, but here on the ice, I started to think that things could be different.

If only I could remember how everything used to be.

Maybe an hour passed. Miss Jessica and Lady Arabella rounded us up to eat dinner on the shore. A few girls stayed behind to talk to

Inger, who had skated far out. They were all just specks of dust in my field of vision.

I sat with a group of girls who were pleasant enough and ate my boxed dinner, mostly keeping to myself. Listening to their conversations passively was entertaining, and I didn't even realize how much time had passed before everyone was finished.

One of Liana's friends, Glenna, started scooping up snow in her hands and melting it in her mouth, claiming it tasted sweeter than sugar. The rest of us followed like lackeys. Somehow, water from the sky did taste a little sweeter here. Maybe it was the lack of distractions or the air, but the Sea was rubbing off on us.

We were all so giddy and distracted we did not see when it happened. Only when Madame Inger came careening onto land did we hear her desperate yelling, the terrible news that she had come to bear.

She was breathless, panting so hard I thought she would collapse. My stomach dropped when she spoke.

"Two girls have fallen through the ice."

***

Luck

I had too many questions, and for once no one was telling me to hold back.

I was excellent on ice, gliding over the smooth floor while frost bit my ears and nose. Madame Inger was coasting a distance away, surrounded by a small group of girls asking questions. I approached them, hoping Liana's bullies were not waiting to chase me away.

"Madame Inger, are you getting married soon?" Cordelia asked, her hands clasped under her chin. "I've been hearing these rumors."

Inger smiled like Cordelia had walked into a mousetrap. "They are false. Do you believe every rumor you hear?"

"Not all of them." Portia adjusted her glasses, snow wetting the lenses. "Like that one about the Burning? Absolute garbage."

"What's it about?" Cordelia asked, her stupid curiosity getting the best of her.

"I don't know. People think it wasn't an accident, that's all." Portia skated away, bumping my shoulder when she passed me.

"Really?" Cordelia looked at me, her eyes wide. "I can't fathom why. The evidence is so clear."

Inger was standing right there. I had heard the rumors too, and none of them said anything good about her.

I shrugged. "I wouldn't be surprised." I looked at my skates, tightening my fists in my pockets. *Inger is right there, you idiot.*

"Huh? What did you say?" Cordelia asked loudly. "You don't think it was an accident? Why?"

"Nothing. Never mind." I turned away, pushing off on one of my skates.

"Wait, Lucienne Legrand." Inger's voice commanded me to stay still. I held my breath.

"Yes, Madame?"

"Tell me what you believe, right here and now." She was staring at me, the cool expression she normally wore replaced by a grimace. The cane in her hand scratched at the ice lazily, carving little caverns in the frozen surface.

"The Burning was an accident. I was just joking." I avoided her eyes. I wanted to get off the ice and join the others.

"Say it again, and this time look at me."

I lifted my head, but my heart could not lie. I had been skeptical of the Burning forever. It was one of those early memories you never really forget.

I had been five or six, watching the fire live on television with Mama and one of the servants. I was never supposed to be up so late, but Mama had let us stay. She had screamed for Maude and me to stop listening and go to our rooms.

But I remembered everything, from the initial reports of an electrical failure causing the fire, even the broadcast where they had declared Princess Isobel Lagarde *missing*, not dead.

"I mean, everyone lies, right?" I muttered, my eyes darting to the sides. "I just meant that I wouldn't be surprised if there was a little bit covered up."

Inger grabbed my neck so suddenly Cordelia screamed. I gasped, the crushing pain only overshadowed by the wave of dread that hit me.

"Do you think you know more than me?"

"No," I choked, tears blurring my vision. *Let me go.*

"Do you think I'm a killer?" she growled, her fingernails pinching my throat. "Do you believe it was all me?"

I was silent. My words could not come fast enough.

"I don't know who told you that, but you won't go around repeating it. I'll make sure." She extended her cane, driving the pointed end into the ice.

"Cordelia, get away," I screamed when Inger let me go, darting to the side. I lost my balance, the cracks spreading too fast for me to escape. They multiplied rapidly, each spiderweb shattering into a million more and making me fall on my side, struggling to find my footing again.

Cordelia tripped too, the weight of her body slamming into the ice starting a chain reaction.

"Help," I yelled, my voice lost to the sound of ice shattering. *It's too early in the season for so much weight on the ice. Was she trying to kill someone?*

Was our future queen the force behind the Burning?

Had everything been a lie?

I did not have time to answer that question. The ice gave out, and I was submerged in merciless, frigid water.

***

Mattie

Lady Arabella showed up to summon me for another meeting, leaving me with no choice but to drop my testing and follow her to Inger's office.

Three days had passed since those girls fell through the ice. There had been a short funeral for one. The palace was painted black, in false mourning since no one even knew the girl personally.

Even the guards we passed were talking about it. Tomas and someone else were deep in conversation. "It was supposed to be fun, Clint. I can't believe someone died. One of those innocent girls."

"Tragedy again," the other said, shaking his head. "This country is cursed."

I could not find Isobel, the most cursed of them all. None of the servants could have told me anything, and I was barred from leaving the palace. I was stuck in meetings or the lab, more miserable than ever.

The office smelled of coffee. Miss Daniels was brewing the stuff in the corner. Norm was cleaning under his nails with a sharp and deadly-looking knife. Not one person gave off a pleasant aura. Joy. For a group so evil, I thought they would find the incident riveting.

Inger crushed her mug in her hands, visibly seething. "The meeting is about to begin."

"But no one is here." I sat down in one of the chairs, plenty of options available.

"Ida and Harry are in Gallen, and Jessica has a class." Inger cleared her throat, officially starting the meeting. "Our plan is about to be compromised."

"Really?" Norm took a sip of coffee, the scent turning my stomach.

"Two students at Etiquette are becoming problems. One of them is obvious; Pizzette Colfer. She needs to be removed from Cyan before she starts talking." Inger wrung the handle of the mug in her hands, muttering to herself. *"The demons come back to haunt me every day."*

"They haunt all of us," Lady Arabella grumbled, sitting back in her chair and resting her heels on the table's surface.

"And there was another student who was looking too far into the Burning. She had the nerve to question me."

"Are we going to terminate them?" Norm asked, tilting up his mug to get the last drops of coffee into his mouth.

"We can't keep killing off Etiquette students," Mr. Daniels coughed out. "The families will start asking questions. This is Cyan, but eventually someone will stand up. Inger, you need to check your temper."

Inger glared at him, and Mr. Daniels immediately knew to stop talking.

"Well how else do you guarantee nothing slips?" Lady Arabella snapped.

"We could always stage a rebel attack," Miss Daniels said, returning with fresh coffee. Norm pounced on the pot, and Arabella was quick to follow. "Say the girls go on another field trip, and the rebels attack them from the shadows. That would take care of our problems."

"Collateral damage, Miscellanea," Mr. Daniels said severely. "Other students might be hurt."

"Since when has that stopped anyone?" Lady Arabella grumbled, taking a long swig of coffee.

Inger nodded, processing this all. "But what about something less unpredictable? I like the idea, but I can't have an uncontained rebel attack. We'd have to hire attackers."

"Why not make up some story about them running away, and then kill them in the woods?" Norm suggested, draining his second cup and filling a third.

Inger shook her head, but I could tell she considered it for a second. We all did.

"Does anyone ever check on Cadmire?" Norm asked out of nowhere. "The hospital's been reporting that he skips days at work, or shows up late, and that's out of the ordinary for him."

"Everything is out of the ordinary for him," Inger snapped.

"You don't think he's about to deviate?" Arabella asked. "Because I'm not about to go looking after him."

I had never met this Cadmire man, but it was clear he was tied into all of this. Just another person in on Inger's agenda.

I wondered if he ever had a choice. If this was what he wanted his life to turn into.

There were choices you never got to make either, so why are you feeling pity for a stranger now?

"I'll keep thinking, but all of you better keep your eyes open. I have to be queen of this miserable country, and a few isolated incidents are not going to ruin that."

***

Luck

I was stuck in a perpetual nightmare for days, plagued by memories I had worked so hard to forget. They came blurry and fast, tumbling over each other and distorting any semblance of clarity. I wanted to scream, but my body failed to respond. Heaviness bogged me down, kept my muscles slack while my eyes refused to open.

Layers of ice trapped me in frigid water, my coat dragging me down. I screamed, pounding my fists against the sheet, seeing only the fractured light and my own face reflected back at me. Terrified. Losing hope every second longer the ice did not budge. I yelled for Maude, Papa. Everyone who had always been there to protect me.

They were elsewhere. Everyone was always elsewhere when I needed them.

The fight left me slowly, retreating into a burning sensation that lasted mere seconds until the blue swallowed me entirely. I did not remember losing consciousness, but at that point I was not sure if my memory worked anymore. If anything did.

I stopped falling, landing hard on my bed at home. My fancy clothes were replaced by a too-short nightgown and slippers, the clothes I wore when it was too hot in the summer and the systems in the house were down.

My bed. I was home, and Papa was in the corner of the room, reading. His face lit up when he saw me, the glimmer in his eyes as bright as they used to be before he and Mama started fighting. I smiled back, though my face felt numb and everything was hazy around the edges. *Papa, there's so much I need to tell you.*

Papa morphed into this blue-clad doctor holding a thermometer and clipboard.

"She's awake and responsive."

I sat up and recoiled from the pain, a sob escaping me. *No, this isn't home. I was supposed to go home.*

"Up the pain relievers. Her senses are coming back."

"Papa?" I managed to whisper, wrapping my arms around myself.

The doctor gave no regards to my question. He examined me up close, his pale eyes sweeping over my frail frame. He adjusted the tubes coming out of my arm and felt around the back of my head for a minute before walking over to the other side of the room.

"Bring in the flashcards. Let's make sure she can still read."

"She's surprisingly competent already—"

"Wait." I reached out toward him, a tremor going through my arms. "The other girl? Cordelia?"

The doctor waved over two physicians. "Can one of you notify her family? They've been pestering us for days on end."

"Hey!" I burst into a coughing fit. One of the doctors ran over, her arm protectively going around my shoulder.

"Rest, Lucienne. Now is not the time to exert yourself."

But a girl died, and I almost did. I'm pretty sure our future queen tried to kill us. No, I'm certain.

I shook my head. "She tried to…"

"Dr. Cadmire, should we put her back to sleep for a little longer?" the doctor asked, patting my shoulder gently.

"No. Madame Inger is coming to this floor later. It would be in our best interest for her to see our efforts have worked. She was against the idea of placing her in a coma."

"Well it worked, doctor. I don't understand how, but it did." The doctor walked away, and it felt like my last confidant had left.

I gave up protesting and laid back against the pillows.

Madame Inger Kaleon had tried to kill me, however unreal the idea seemed, because I was skeptical about the Burning. It was a crime not to be, especially with how stringent security was here, and how vacant the palace grounds felt. And because of me, Cordelia had perished. For some reason, I did not follow.

Inger was hiding something about the Burning she did not want anyone looking into. I was beginning to think an entire network of lies was going on right over our heads.

If there was one thing I would accomplish during my time at Etiquette, it would be to uncover each and every lie.

***

Mattie

It was the most intense, dragged-out week of my life.

Inger was on edge. After her explosion on ice, little rumors had started to circulate around the noble families, especially those close to Cordelia Len. In the northern towns, rebels had been filmed setting fire to the Cyan flag and banners with Inger's face printed on them. Of course, that news rarely reached the city's people, but all of us in the palace got to see it live. Every day was another conflict, another disagreement.

Inger called another meeting, probably to end the cycle of everyone silently acknowledging each other while we crept around the palace. I put more time into my work in the lab, sometimes taking my notes outside to avoid her and Lady Arabella's prying and delay attending meetings.

I sat under a tree on the hardened snow, my notebook spread across my lap. I studied other subjects when I was not in the lab, just to keep my mind busy. What else was there to do?

I could not focus. Sitting here bundled up nicely while Isobel needed help and people were dying was wrong. Running away would never be as simple as it played out in my head. I once overheard Harry telling someone it was impossible for anyone on Inger's team to get away from her. If we strayed too far off the grid, she somehow had a way of knowing. So, I was stuck here, pretending my life was okay and that I was not scared of being a witness to more bloodshed we were supposed to have left behind after the Burning. No, long before that, when the world had almost dissolved into nothingness over war.

"Lady Matilda?"

I looked over my shoulder. "'Oh, hello, Tomas."

"Why are you out here all alone?" He hovered by the doorway for a second, and then abandoned the spot, taking a couple steps closer to me.

"I just wanted to study where no one would bother me." I closed the book, sliding it under my leg and crossing my arms. The pretty gowns and circlet that belonged to Lady Matilda were tucked away somewhere in my closet. I was Mattie again, with my ratty cloak, worn slippers, and messy hair. I wondered how Tomas could still call me by my false title with a straight face. "You can call me Mattie by the way." *I already told you.*

"Okay." He came and sat by me. Neither of us spoke for a minute, then he shrugged. "It's quieter here. It feels like no one is watching."

"That's why I like it." I rested my chin on my knuckles, staring off at the school building in the distance. "And Inger doesn't come out back a lot."

"Are you avoiding her? I thought you were part of her circle." He shuffled around to face me, disturbing the snow at our feet.

"How could you possibly think that was real?" I tipped my head to the side, raising an eyebrow. "I'm wearing dirty clothes, my hair is a mess, and I haven't gone out in days. Nothing about me screams Royal Advisor."

Tomas's eyes darted to the side, his cheeks reddening. "Honestly, I never notice those things about you."

I sucked my cheeks in, wondering why he looked so bashful. My head was starting to hurt, every second longer he sat there sending my body into overdrive, like it was not sure how to handle his presence. My heart was racing, and my stomach was fluttering. My palms were clammy though it was below freezing, and my hands were ungloved. All tied to some emotions I did not have a name for.

"What do you notice then?"

He scratched the back of his head, blushing even more. "Your eyes. They're a different shade of blue than what you normally see in Cyan. And your hair…it's red like mine, but deeper." He let out a tense breath. "I'm not making any sense."

"It's okay. I think I understand." I did not, but he was trying so hard to be cordial that I had to meet him halfway.

"You're different, but in a good way."

That struck me somewhere deep, my pulse speeding up. *Why do I feel so strange? Like I...I don't know. I don't know what to call this feeling.*

"Thank you," I whispered, biting the tip of my nail to stop myself from rambling. I stared down at our feet, still on some kind of high without a reason.

"You're welcome." More quiet seconds passed, but this time it felt fine. The air was calmer than it had been for weeks, and it was just the two of us, sitting side by side and breathing it in. Every cold breath seemed to wake me up, doing little to stop the burning inside me. When the wind blew, my tangled hair ended up in Tomas's face, and he was too polite to complain.

"Were you trying to call me pretty?" I asked, pushing my thumb up against my chin. *Why does asking him such a simple question feel so strange?*

Tomas's reaction mirrored my internal battle. He straightened his back, letting out a sheepish laugh. "Well, yeah. Lady...Mattie. I was getting there."

The corners of my mouth lifted. I could not remember the last time I had smiled and felt something genuine inside. Happiness. "Thank you, Tomas."

He nodded, whispering something and bowing his head. His left knee was bouncing up and down, snow spreading all around our shoes.

"It's rather cold today." I rubbed my hands together, crossing my ankles. "I wish it would snow again."

Without a warning, Tomas threw an arm over my shoulder, pulling me so close I could hear his heart in my ear.

There it goes again. My heart won't settle down.

"What are you doing?"

"You said you were cold. I'm warming you up."

"Oh." Maybe it was a hug in reality, and I was missing the cue. I did not have any friends in the parts of my childhood I remembered. No parents or anyone to call a guardian. Inger Kaleon was not the type to take any of those places.

I patted his elbow, a poor attempt at completing the gesture. "This feels nice." *Nice? I was getting so worked up about feeling nice?*

"It does," he said in a low voice, the soft fabric of his coat squashed up against my face.

If life could feel this nice for everyone, then maybe people would never have gone to war in the first place. Made the same mistake four times and learned nothing. Tomas's hug brought me back to a place where I still thought everything was possible, a place where I could simply exist in peace.

Forget about all the evil I was only inclined to witness but never do anything to stop.

"Matilda," Lady Arabella said from behind us. "What are you doing?"

"Studying," I said as casually as I could, letting go of Tomas. "He was keeping me warm. I called him over."

Lady Arabella did not even look at Tomas. "Go inside, kid, or else I'll have Norm speak to you."

"Yes, ma'am." Tomas stood up, brushing the snow off his pant legs. Before he left, he squeezed my shoulder. The nice feeling lingered there.

Lady Arabella watched until he was gone, then faced me, her eyes severe. "Come on. Inger called another meeting, and you're late."

I know. I planned it that way.

I followed her to the office, already missing the few minutes of peace I had outside with Tomas. He had some kind of effect on me that I liked.

Miss Daniels was the only person standing, brewing a pot of coffee in the corner. Norm had two cups of the stuff next to him, his eyes bloodshot and furious. Inger had her feet up on the table, her usual ugly palace gowns swapped for a more off-putting green dress. She yawned, tossing her head back and barely acknowledging me.

"We need supporters," she started, covering her mouth to yawn again. I found my chair, pulling my feet up off the ground and onto the seat. "I think we should go to the poorest town in Cyan."

Pigladen. Next to me, Norm grunted as he downed another cup of coffee. Lady Arabella wrinkled her nose, clearly bothered by the idea.

"We shall tell the students that two of them will be selected for a diplomatic observation opportunity, specifically, our two problems at the school: Colfer and Legrand. During the observation, we will simply pay off a group of rebels to handle the job for us. As children of the upper ranks, they'll be easy targets for those pig-headed people."

"What about Isobel?" Norm asked, completely glossing over the fact Inger had so calmly discussed her plans for murdering two students. Their disregard for life was sickening, but I could not claim to be better. After all, I was still sitting amongst them.

"She's coming with us, simply because my testing is complete. The girl is ungifted." Inger reached for one of Norm's cups, taking a sip without blinking an eye.

Ungifted? What is she talking about?

"And we can slip her in with the students. The rebels won't mind one extra, weak, and pathetic girl." Inger met each of our eyes. "That's the outline. Of course, the plan becomes more intricate as time goes on."

I did not want to be part of this. The nice feelings I had earlier on were gone, replaced by dread and despair. I had to find Isobel. If there was anything my life had to offer, it was not helping this witch become queen. Even Pizzette and Lucienne needed my help now. I would have to risk something. It was not right for me to be here while their lives were in danger.

"Does it bother you that it took us so long to find Isobel?" Lady Arabella asked, cracking her knuckles. "For eight years, there wasn't a single trace of the girl, like she'd disappeared with the ashes, and we couldn't do a thing about it."

"Of course, it bothers me." Inger shook her head, furious. "After all these years, the girl just waltzed into the police station. Marlene Selle was taunting us. The whole time she's been living in the city, working under our noses and hiding this from us."

Marlene Selle was also no longer alive. I was sitting next to her killers.

"No longer. Cyan will soon be yours, Inger," Norm muttered, staring into Inger's eyes. "Soon, and very soon."

Not if I could find the courage to stop them.

***

Pizzette

It was another ordinary day of class because no one cared enough about the two students missing from our classes to let it show on their faces.

We had all gone to Cordelia Len's funeral. Liana and her crew cried fake tears and put on sad faces, claiming they were close to the girl's family. I stood with the rest of our school, not pretending the bagpipes and eulogy brought genuine tears out of me. Sometimes, sadness and fear manifested itself in different ways. I did not need to sob for anyone to know I felt something. It was visible in the little tremors in my hands and my absent voice.

There were no questions when Luck returned to History a few days later. She looked perfectly fine, which did not fit the last image I had of her unconscious in the snow with a team of doctors surrounding her, icicles clinging to her hair.

Even with our tainted past, I was happy that she was alright.

Lady Arabella walked into the classroom with a pile of pamphlets in her hands. "Good afternoon. These are informational guides for an upcoming diplomatic observation opportunity for two students."

I mentally checked out, turning to stare out the window. It was refusing to snow. Cyan could not decide on a consistent weather pattern. It was tiresome, seeing the same gray sky and lazy rain mixed with ice falling for a few minutes at a time.

"In light of some recent rebel activity in the outer provinces, Madame Inger is planning a peace-offering means for communication. Two students will accompany her team over the winter holiday to participate in speeches and assemblies. The goal is to show the people of Pigladen and other troubled towns that the city of Cyan is still looking out for the rest of the country. We haven't reverted to our old ways if our young students support our leader. If you are interested, raise your hand and I will give you a pamphlet to read."

It was so clear no one cared when not a single hand moved.

Lady Arabella sighed. "There's scholarship money involved."

"How much?" Liana asked, leaning onto her standing desk.

"Half a million cizotes."

"Oh, I don't know…"

"Two million for each student." I did not need the money, but when everyone was suddenly interested and raised their hands, I almost joined in.

I was done with Inger. I did not want to spend any time outside my winter holiday anywhere but on my makeshift bed in our empty mansion, messaging my friends in Bark and stuffing my face with sugar while trying to find clues about Inger's shady past.

Lady Arabella came down the aisles, dropping papers on everyone's desks. She stopped in front of mine, her hand hovering over my desk.

"Yes?"

"What is the name of your digital bank account? It was never entered into the system." She narrowed her eyes at me, the rest of the class staring as well. "You were present the first day, correct?"

I nodded, and then remembered I had snuck out.

I left them a humongous clue on accident. The identity of the girl who snuck in and out of Etiquette was not so hard to name now.

"It's Telize, ma'am."

Her brows wrinkled. "Your last name is Colfer. What is Telize supposed to be?"

"It's just the name of my family's bank account." I wished there was a chair for me to sink into.

"You could have told me that weeks ago, when the rest of the school did. Try to evade paying school fees again, and you will be expelled." She left two papers on my desk and continued onto the next row.

I shoved them in my bag, my face burning up in shame. I was always making a fool of myself. Trying to be independent and stick up for myself always ended in me getting embarrassed, looking like the only girl who missed the memo to act within reason.

I noticed Lady Arabella having another conversation with Luck. At least theirs was not about some bank account name.

Just a few more days, then you can get out of here and hopefully never return.

Mattie

I packaged a hundred doses of Preserv into small packets, wishing I could fake an accident and get them destroyed. If it were not for the camera Norm had installed two nights ago, I would have done that and moved on. Inger had her small collection and those red pills. She had not even let me test to make sure the Preserv worked.

I hoped I failed miserably, and that the menace of my lifetime would not keep living forever.

"Matilda." Lady Arabella's disinterested voice could be recognized from anywhere.

"Another meeting?" I asked, spinning around on my stool. I nearly lost my balance and fell when I saw who Lady Arabella silently brought into my lab.

No. How could she be here?

Isobel Lagarde was standing beside her, surprisingly clean and wearing a dark blue dress. The hood Inger had mentioned was moved up a few inches, revealing the face I hoped I would never see in Inger's clutches. The pictures I processed were almost a perfect match, but they were lacking the life in her eyes, the tremulous aura the little girl radiated.

I pressed three fingers to my temple, another headache starting. "What is it? Why is she here?"

"They're planning a trip to Pigladen. Petrakova is only in attendance because she is one of the servants we are bringing along. The others already heard the message." Lady Arabella knew I could see through her lies. There would be no other servants, and there was nothing left to add to the plan.

Inger wanted to make sure I knew she had won. This was a game to her, psyching me out before I could try and grab the princess and run. The heir to the throne of Cyan would be sitting right across from me, completely oblivious, and if I spoke up, Norm, or someone else, would kill both of us right there.

She wanted me to decide. *Isobel or me? To please Inger, it has to be me. I have to be selfish and choose to protect myself.*

"Hurry up, Mattie. Don't just sit there gawking." Lady Arabella pushed Isobel's shoulder forward. The princess took a few wobbly steps toward the door, probably in awe of the false opportunity she was getting. The poor girl never had the life she was meant to have. A princess, especially one as coveted and adored as her, did not grow up in hiding and work in the shadows. They were meant to live above it all, as domineering as the stars. Inger had stolen that from her.

"Yes, ma'am." I slid off the stool, falling in line behind them. We walked through the halls in a pod, none of us speaking a word to each other. When we passed a group of guards and I saw Tomas was with them, I turned my head to the side, too ashamed of myself to look at him.

Inger's office was full of vibrant energy. Miss Jessica had finally showed up and was chatting with Mr. and Miss Daniels while Norm and Inger were whispering to each other, their elbows touching. Even without Harry and Ida, this group was whole. They did not need help complementing each other's madness.

The talk died down when we walked in with Isobel between us. Mr. Daniels averted his eyes, most likely remembering the roles they must have played in the death of her family and the destruction of her home. Miss Daniels pursed her lips, scratching her hand obsessively. Miss Jessica glanced at Inger across the table, who was gripping Norm's arm and trying to keep her face calm.

Just for a second, I wanted them to face what they had done, no matter how uncomfortable it made them feel.

"Hello, all. Let's begin our discussion." Lady Arabella pointed to a chair for Isobel. She was so small compared to the rest of us. Instead of placing her feet on the ground or as close as she could get them, she sat on her knees, resting her elbows on the table.

My head pulsed, making my chest feel heavy. She looked like a giddy little kid about to receive a gift.

Inger clapped her hands together, giving up on smiling. "There is much unrest in the poorer towns, as you all know. The burning of the Cyan flag and my image shows that there is a disconnect between us and our people. That is why we are having this diplomatic observation venture happen. Two students and a handful of servants will accompany us to these towns where we will deliver speeches and spread goodwill. Assure the rest of the country that we are all still unified through tragedy."

Tragedy you caused.

Next to me, Isobel squirmed on her seat, probably confused as to why someone so young was even a part of this adult conversation. I could not even pretend she would be safe. I could not come up with words to reassure her.

Norm was studying her face, as if he expected some kind of reaction. Lucky for him, I learned, the concoction she'd been given had erased any memories she might have of his face, or the terrible way she ended up at the palace. Isobel watched him too, but I noticed her eyes never lingered on one person for long. She was building a profile of everyone.

"We shall be leaving December twenty-sixth. After Christmas Eve mass, Lady Arabella will tell the two girls we have selected to come with us that they must pack a light bag and wear the uniforms we shall provide. It should be a smooth journey. No bumps in the road."

Everyone nodded. Lady Arabella stood up, taking Isobel's hand. "That is all you need to hear, Petrakova. It's time to go back to work."

Isobel did not protest, but she did slip her hand out of Lady Arabella's once they were through the door. The second it closed, Inger started talking to Norm, ignoring the rest of us.

"Why were you looking at her so much?" she asked, her voice hitching up an octave. The sound shield had to be working twice as hard now.

"I couldn't shake the feeling that she remembered me. All of us." Norm shrugged, clasping his big hands together.

"That's impossible. Dr. Cadmire ran several tests when we first brought her in, and then gave her a plethora of drugs. A few seconds of your face in the woods is no longer ingrained in her memory. She's probably forgotten Marlene Selle as well."

"Is that it?" Miss Jessica asked, leaning closer to Norm.

"She looks like Cyrana, that's all," Norm admitted.

"Well, that face won't be around much longer," Inger snapped, tearing her eyes from Norm's.

Witch. You take everything you can get your hands on.

In that moment I decided that, no matter the cost, I would stop being her Advisor. This diplomatic nonsense would be my opportunity to finally defy her.

Then I was going to set Isobel free.

***

Pizzette

Winter holiday came faster than I dreamt. I spent the last day of classes taking exams and itching to get outside and run home if I had to. Instead, we were instructed to go to our rooms, put on our fanciest dresses and cloaks, and head to the church as a class.

I guess everyone here doesn't bring anything home with them. Maybe all these dresses look the same after a while. I tossed on a plain red gown and indulged in my nice boots and faux fur cloak, tying my hair back with a big white bow. My diamond hung down, a bit of sparkle in my otherwise dreary life.

We walked across a path shoveled by servants into the city, the cold making my nose and fingers numb. New students like me were talking excitedly behind their hands, probably expecting this trip into the city to be a treat. We ended up less than a block away inside a large and gray stone church that was as somber and plain as the rest of the country. Everyone found it enchanting.

The classes filed into pews sectioned off for us. The rest of the attendants at the Christmas Eve mass were watching from their pews and galleries, the altar at the center of it all, looking more like a stage for a performance. Their faces were scrutinizing, probably disapproving of all of us loud and unruly young ladies with no class.

Another school's students filled the section across the aisle from ours, young men who all looked like they were frozen on magazine covers, with perfect hair and suits and faces. Even me, usually uninterested in lusting over strangers, could not help but peek at them.

"They're from Drusseau College, on the other side of the city," Liana whispered to someone in front of us. "They're all rich bachelors from all over the world. Drusseau is one of the top schools for boys."

"Why do they have to be separated from us?" I asked, still looking occasionally. *I swear, those guys are not real.*

"Because Cyans don't encourage anything that makes young life exciting." Liana frowned, flipping her hair over her shoulder and waving at one of them. "I hate it sometimes. My parents don't want me to go to Principles, where everyone studies together."

"You'll have to meet a husband one day," Ellen said with a smirk. "You'll grow up not even knowing how to hold his hand."

"That's why you practice at parties and at Christmas Eve balls." Liana adjusted the collar of her cloak, looking completely flustered. "So, you don't embarrass yourself when you're older."

I did not see much sense in Cyan's system, but I kept my mouth shut. The pianos started playing, and everyone stood up and started to sing.

All of the hymns were in French. It was a good thing I had not bothered to study for my French exam and barely passed. I was not the only person mumbling through the pages.

"I barely stayed awake in French," someone behind me muttered. "I do this every year, but now everyone is staring at us."

It was true. The entire congregation, including the priest, had one eye on us throughout the entire mass. It was only towards the end, when a familiar chord struck my ears, did I stop focusing on their heavy gaze.

Everyone was singing one of my favorite songs from home, but every word was in French.

When we were finally let loose, I nearly ran out of there to escape the awkward atmosphere and the music I felt like I was not supposed to be a part of making.

Cabs were waiting outside for us in a chaotic fashion, mixed in with limousines and cars from the rest of the churchgoers. I waited with the others, feeling like a project on display while the guys from Drusseau walked by and glanced at us.

"We'll see you at our party," Penny squealed, waving at the boys. She turned to the rest of us, overly excited. "You're all invited too. Our mansion in Tumbleweed Gardens is big enough for the whole city."

I was not interested in a party on Christmas Eve. Usually, I opened presents and ate dozens of sweets and fell asleep watching movies with Mom. I was not aware of any plans she made this year.

I spotted her leaving hand in hand with someone else. Before she left through the doors, she remembered she had a child to pick up and whirled around, her face elated and distracted. The man seemed to laugh with her, casually slipping his hand around her waist as he followed her gaze.

My stomach turned. *Who is he?*

I left the group, giving my companions a half smile before crossing the lobby. The man left Mom's side long enough to let her hug me.

"Pizzette, I missed you," she whispered in my ear, shaking with joy. "It's been a long month, right?"

"Yeah." *I almost got killed by this guard and found out you let a doctor run trials on my memory. Oh, and our future queen is insane. Good to see you too.* "Who's this guy?"

"Oh." Mom smiled warmly. "This is—"

"Papa!" *Lucienne Legrand* ran across the room and into the man's arms.

The pieces put themselves together rather quickly.

I turned to my mother, her smile dropping once she saw my face.

"Pizzette, wait—"

"You're with *him*?"

***

Luck

I forgot about my anger once I jumped into Papa's arms. All the emotions I had been bottling up for a month spilled out. I sobbed into his shoulder, clutching the back of his jacket and hurrying through my tales. "It's *awful*. Everyone bullies me and then I almost drowned and…" I felt a stab of pain when I remembered he had not been waiting for me when I woke up. No one had. But he was here now. That had to mean something.

"Lucienne, you're okay," Papa whispered, kissing the top of my head. "I'm so sorry I couldn't come up and visit you. My heart stopped the moment we received the phone call. Your mother was supposed to be there."

"Mama?" I wiped my eyes with the back of my hand, anger burning inside me. I wanted to ask him where he had been hiding but seeing the emotion on his face stopped me. He was truly sorry. "Let me drop out of Etiquette, Papa. Please. That place will flood me with fire."

"Lucienne…" He shook his head, squeezing my shoulders once. "I'm so sorry. I'm so sorry you're stuck there."

"I'll go somewhere out of the city, or study at home." My voice sharpened, tears coming again. "Please, Papa."

"We've put a lot of time and money into Etiquette. You can't just drop out after a month."

It always came down to money in my family. *I shouldn't have expected him to understand. If I died, he'd be looking for a way to be refunded for my wasted education.*

I turned away from him, staring down at my shoes. "Are we going home for Christmas? Where is Mama? Maude?"

Papa's voice barely sounded in my ears. "Lucky, this year is going to be different for our family."

My eyes darted up. He almost never called me by my nickname. "What do you mean?"

Papa shifted his gaze to the woman standing a few feet away. I knew her immediately.

Pizzette Colfer's mother, Edith.

"Papa, explain yourself. I don't understand." But I did. I was not a child anymore. Mama and Papa had been fighting for so long, and I saw him with another woman in the snow.

An affair. My father was having an affair with this awful woman.

I whirled around and slammed my fist into his shoulder. "How could you? How could you do this to our perfect family?" I cried, punching him harder with every word. I thought his abandonment and disregard for my safety was the limit. No. He did not even have the decency to tell me in private. "You told me it was nothing that day at the gala. You promised me you wouldn't let anyone come into our family and break us apart."

Papa pulled me into his arms, stifling my yelling in his shoulder. "Lucky, I'm sorry. I didn't know how to tell you."

"And you picked that witch?" I snapped, pushing against him. "You picked *her* over Mama?"

"Let's not make a scene," Edith said quietly. "We can take a cab back to my house. I've prepared dinner."

I did not want to go anywhere with her. Papa swiveled me around and marched me outside. We got into the first cab to arrive and sped off, distancing ourselves from the drama I created inside.

Papa skipped the passenger seat and sat next to me, an invisible wall between us. No words were exchanged for the first fifteen minutes, and then he started trying to explain in French so the driver would not understand. I was still too far from being fluent, so I just let the words hover in the air until he changed his mind.

"I swear I was going to tell you. I've been talking to Edith for months now, but we only recently decided to move forward. She came to Cyan for many reasons, but one of them was me."

An invisible fist choked my heart. I sniffled, digging my nails into my arms. "Do Mama and Maude know? Have you updated the rest of *our* family?"

"Your mother has known. Maude…I'll tell her when she returns."

"From where?"

"Gallen. Her trip will last a few days longer, then she'll be home. I know you miss her."

I did miss my sister. She deserved to be eating dinner with us, not annoying Pizzette and her backwoods mother.

"Luck look at me," Papa whispered.

I crossed my arms, staring out the window. It was getting dark, holiday lights turning on automatically. It felt like ages had passed since I left the palace compound. Life had gone on without me.

"Lucky, please."

We were among the wealthiest and classiest members of society, yet we were also one of the most deceptive and deceitful families. Being Lady Lucienne had never felt so much like a curse.

The cab stopped outside an older mansion in Tumbleweed Gardens, blocks from our property. I dashed out of the car and through the gate without Papa, hoping he understood that I did not want to speak to him anymore.

We still ended up side by side waiting for Edith to open the door. Somehow, she and Pizzette had returned before us, probably because our cab driver had taken the most predictable and crowded route. The door opened, and artificial light and happiness hit me like a tidal wave.

"Hello. You and Luck missed Lady Arabella's announcement," Edith said, pulling Papa inside by his wrist. "Both of our girls were selected for the diplomatic observation opportunity."

The news did little to help my mood. I trudged in behind them, slamming the door shut.

The mansion was old and dusty, though Edith had tried to clean it without the help of servants. The furniture was embarrassingly small and cheap, as though it had been purchased in the past two weeks. The dining room we were supposed to be reclining in hardly had enough space for the four of us. I could not fathom how a home could be so large, empty, and crowded at the same time.

Or maybe I saw it all as horrid because I would rather be anywhere else but here.

"Look, I'm just as annoyed as you are," Pizzette hissed in my ear as she walked past, securing a seat as far away from me as possible. "About everything."

At least she had not known either. I sat diagonally from her, leaving Papa and Edith to pick the last two opposing spots. Pizzette seemed to be enjoying how awkward she had made the situation.

"I know this is rather sudden," Papa started to say as he sat next to Pizzette, killing the smirk on her face. "But Edith and I couldn't wait anymore. We thought this quiet night would be an appropriate time to break the news to you both."

On what planet? I rolled my eyes, inching my chair away from Edith. I did not need her dust and poverty rubbing off on me.

"We've known each other since you girls were young," Edith said. "And we reconnected last year."

Pizzette seemed to go pale. I did not miss her hands grabbing for her diamond necklace.

"And although we made some mistakes and thought separating was for the better, we have decided to join again." Papa cleared his throat, looking across the table at Edith with admiration in his eyes. "The past is gone."

The past was my entire childhood and life with two parents I thought loved each other. *Glad to see it meant a lot to you too, Papa.*

"We want to try and make this work. Us, living as a family," Edith said, giving Pizzette and I pointed looks. "Are you willing to try?"

"Hell no." I stood up and left the dining room, sick to my stomach. After everything, this was not how I had expected going home to be. My house, my family, and my happiness, all sacrificed to Papa's affair. I would not sit there and pretend I was fine with it.

***

Pizzette

Luck's abrupt departure was an invitation for me to do the same. I did not bother to look at the ring Sir Legrand pulled out before I also ran to my room.

I locked the door, falling on my bed, stupidly expensive gown, shoes, and all. I was not crying. I just lay there quietly, breathing in air and slowly letting it out. I found myself squeezing my diamond without thinking again, the cool silver against my rough hands calming. I did not even have the chance to ask Mom about my father's death or the memory-erasing surgery. After the display downstairs, it was clear she had already moved on. What she cared about was the ring around her finger, not the man who had been a part of our family before fate took him away, or the doctor who liked to hide forcing his memory out of my head without permission. And she came back to Cyan after everything, not to try and find him and restore my memory, but to get married to Sir Louis Legrand and move in with him. Start a new family and start over without me on board.

The emotions inside me were too new, too raw. I stroked my old blanket, inhaling the smell of Bark wood smoke that would be forever embedded in it. How I wished I could lay here forever, with my father and home close to my heart.

But Cyan was the replacement. I was going to be here a long time, trapped in the lies and misery and pain. Wondering if my future queen would order my death because I snuck out. Wondering if I would ever make a single friend here. Wondering if I would ever stop feeling like I was stuck between two worlds I technically would never belong in.

My mother did not care. She was the one who brought me here.

It was that thought that made me get up and check her room. It used to be a place I could go to whenever, because there were no secrets between us. Just the two of us, and we were happy.

The door to her room was closed, and I did not have the motivation to open it when I remembered where she was.

I guess I'll just go back downstairs. It won't get any better if I wander around my own house.

I heard Mom and Sir Legrand panicking before I even got to the bottom of the stairs. Apparently, after Luck had stormed away, she'd had a panic attack in the guest bathroom and was currently screaming at her father to take them home. No one noticed me in the background.

I was glad when Christmas Eve was finally over.

***

Inger stared out of her office window, a mug of coffee in her hand. She was beginning to understand Arabella, who claimed she spent too much time sulking in there alone. At least it was soundproof, and there was no one to witness her ranting and screaming obscenities while avoiding sleep.

It began to snow, turning the morning of December twenty-sixth into mud. The pretty snow quickly turned into ugly slush once the cars started running again, throwing the powdery white into oblivion.

They would be leaving today. Three coaches were already waiting in the driveway. Inger packed her favorite knife between the folds of her clothes, making sure it was immaculate. There would always be a failsafe if the initial plan did not work. *Cadmire could have thought of that.*

Someone entered the room, much to her annoyance since she had not felt anyone approaching. *Still too weak. Maybe that Preserv doesn't work after all.*

Arabella stood behind her, trailed by two miserable creatures. "It's almost time, Inger."

Inger nodded, a whirlwind roaring inside of her. She tried not to look at her niece. It would be harder to kill her if her face was always on Inger's mind.

The other girl held a package of Preserv capsules, her shoulders hunched and countenance frail. It would be hard to dispose of her as well. In another life, Mattie could have been like a daughter to her. Maybe come to see the world from Inger's eyes instead of judging her with that damaged mind.

Oh well. Inger had one life, and it was already half-wasted.

***

Luck

I mumbled goodbye to Papa and Mama and stepped into the car going to the palace with a little bag of clothes. The whole ride there was like a death march with a finite distance to my destination, the bumps in the road the only irregular pattern tearing me from my dread-filled thoughts.

I had not told either of my parents the truth I was struggling to believe myself. Some awful part of me did not think they would care to listen, not when so many problems were going on at home. Not when they were fighting with each other and cheating and so much more.

No one had been in the hospital when I woke up. No one was going to be listening to me today.

Now I was walking right into Inger's home, armed with nothing but a bank account and a famous last name. I knew I had no way of stopping her by myself, but I accepted the trip only to spite her. Somehow, I was going to expose her for what she had done. It would give my sadness some meaning.

Lady Matilda met me outside the palace. She was wearing the same clothes I first saw her in, the same strained smile still on her face.

"Hello, Lucienne. Come inside. I'll get your clothes."

"Luck," I mumbled, dragging my bag behind me. No one came to carry it. There did not seem to be anyone alive here. The inside of the palace was every bit as magnificent and terrifying as rumors said, with all the shadows and empty hallways reminding me of what was never coming back.

"Mattie," she said, broadening her grin. "You can get changed in this room. Pizzette is already here."

Always stumbling a step ahead of me. I slipped into the bathroom, my head still throbbing from my panic attack two days earlier. It scared me that it had come out of nowhere, something I had not dealt with for years. I hoped whatever transpired in the next few days would not bring back the fears of my past.

A hideous gray dress was laid out on the counter, the white polka dots looking more like targets. I stuffed my clothes away, hoping the uniform phase would wear out after the first day. If I was going to be dressed like anyone else, I had to have a say in how I looked.

I walked out into the hall. Pizzette appeared from around a corner, sporting a black backpack and running shoes. I scoffed at her choice of style. Though she was Edith's annoying daughter, there was something admirable about her temperament. She was talking to an older guard, looking plenty enthralled in whatever he had to say.

"Really? Inger has never taken students on her diplomatic trips?" she asked, pulling the straps even higher up on her shoulders.

"Inger never even takes diplomatic trips. No one likes her."

"I wish someone had told me that earlier. I would've told the driver he was mistaken." Pizzette playfully punched his shoulder. "Tomas, you need to keep me in the loop."

Mattie seemed to be hovering around them, unsure of what to say. My presence gave her some inspiration.

"It's time to go to Inger's office. I guess we'll be seeing you later, Tomas." She waved, but it was the most stilted and rehearsed wave I had ever seen, like she had to practice it in some dark room first.

The guard smiled, but there was a warning look in his eyes. "Be careful, Mattie. I don't know what she has planned."

"And me," Pizzette laughed nervously. "Luck too."

Tomas did not notice her. He had eyes for Mattie only, and the girl barely noticed. I fell in line behind them, wondering if Inger's plans had something to do with a large sheet of floating ice.

Don't be scared. Stare your enemy in the eye and tackle them head on.

I had to find out more about Inger's games. Cyan was my home after all, and even with my family falling apart, I would not let the world go down along with it.

Mattie led us into a small office teeming with strangers. None of them were in a hurry to introduce themselves, so I had to fill in the holes.

Inger, Lady Arabella, and Miss Jessica. Those were the only faces I knew, then I noticed the little girl peering out the window.

My mouth lifted into a smile. "Petrakova, it's me."

She turned around slowly. Though I had only seen part of her face before, the vibrant eyes were unforgettable. Now her entire head was uncovered, revealing pretty black curls and a face that resonated somewhere inside my mind. Maybe I had seen her more than I remembered.

"Luck!" She crossed the room and took my hands, spinning me in a circle. "You're coming too."

"Yeah." There was so much life in the small hands gripping mine. I prayed someone would protect her from the horrors that had caught up to me.

"Hey." Pizzette knelt next to her, studying her carefully. "I know you. You're that kid who I carried stuff for."

Petrakova's smile grew even bigger. "What's your name?"

"Pizzette. And yours it Petrakova?" She nodded. "That's a very pretty name."

Petrakova's eyes sparkled. She held both of our hands, radiating joy. "Now I have two friends who will help me!"

I had no idea what she meant. My heart ached when she admitted we were her only two friends. Pizzette had not even known her name. Her *Marmi* was still out of the picture, and it did not seem appropriate to ask anything about her.

Inger interrupted our reunion. "I see you all know each other?" she asked in an icy voice.

Pizzette answered for all of us. "Somehow. Like we're connected or something."

"Ha," Inger said blankly, walking past us and pulling Mattie toward the door. "Come on, girls. The coaches are waiting."

***

Mattie

I was crawling all over with chills, the nice feeling I held onto since seeing Tomas in the hallway replaced with dread. It was impossible to relax with the three cars processing out of Cyan, possibly for forever. Pizzette and Luck were stuck with Norm in the last car. The Daniels and Miss Jessica rode in the second. I was trapped in the lead car with Inger, Lady Arabella, and Isobel Lagarde.

Inger had soundproofed the back two sections of the car and set a sight shield, so the driver was oblivious of what was happening behind him. I mentally pleaded for him to help me anyway.

"Now we know what we are really here to do," Inger grumbled. The hidden message went right over Isobel's head.

"The event is scheduled for tomorrow at noon. Our problems will be taken care of." Lady Arabella rubbed her hands together to warm them. "I want to get out of Pigladen as soon as possible."

Tonight. I had to free them tonight.

I clutched the side of my head, overwhelmed. "Wait, where are we staying? The accommodations?"

Inger glanced at me, barely interested. "Three shacks. They don't build anything big enough in Pigladen for the whole group."

I kept a smile off my face. I touched my cheeks with my fingertips, feeling something nice and warm glowing beneath them. Happy. I thought that the news had made me happy.

Isobel caught my eye and waved, still oblivious as to what was going to happen. She would find out soon enough. I did not know how she would react, being so small. Would she even comprehend what I was telling her? *I don't want to elaborate on the awful details of her past, but she might not willingly come with us if she's unconvinced.*

I nodded to them, then pressed my forehead against the window, letting the coolness calm my headache. I could do this. I could save Isobel and the rest of the girls. Maybe even Cyan.

I was never included in that group, but I was beginning to be fine with it.

***

Luck

Pigladen, that disgusting place.

I swore in my head as we trundled through the rusting iron gates that marked the border of Pigladen.

I cringed as the townspeople arrived. They came in hordes despite the hour, slapping the sides of the car and shouting unintelligible words. I picked up on some French and bits of other languages, but nothing seemed cohesive. They were ragged, rail-thin with ashy and pale skin, wearing washed out shirts and ripped leggings, their feet bare and blistered, and covered with sand. Their voices were as angry as their hands as they beat against the cars.

Pizzette sat next to me while the man called Norm sat across from us, looking indifferent. Pizzette was as gray as her dress, pressing her thumbs against her diamond and focusing on that. I thought of the large breakfast I had eaten, and the mansion I would be returning to. In the dwindling light, we passed sorry excuses for homes and dirty wells. There were not even any paved roads. We had uneaten lunch sitting in boxes on the empty seat, the smell of baked chicken and potatoes intoxicating. I wanted to hand them out to the masses but stayed seated. Norm's stare was pinning me in place.

We drove through the crowded, muddy streets. The smell of sweat and disease filled my nose. There were ragged people crowding around a mud puddle, scooping it up and drinking it with their hands. Pizzette covered her face with her hands.

"I'm not used to this. That may come as a surprise to you," she muttered. "Seeing this amount of suffering sickens me."

"Me too." I swiped sweat off my forehead, nerves and disgust making me ill. "Norm, why is it so warm here? It's the middle of winter."

He had not spoken to us the entire day, but now his eyes fixated on us so intensely I nearly fell out of the chair. "It's a manufactured climate, used in other parts of the world to establish growing regions. It was part of the Environment Restoration Act."

"I guess it's bad enough here without the winter," Pizzette breathed. "Not even a drop a clean water or a spot of fertile soil to farm."

"They have the river, stupidly named Mudlark Moat. It crosses the boundary between climates and sometimes freezes over." Norm shook his head, losing patience with us. Perhaps it was best if we stayed quiet for the rest of the journey.

I could not help myself. "And we're staying here for a few days? We'll end up dehydrated, or sick with cholera." I brushed my hands against the ugly gray dress, the polka dots over my knees luminescent in the dark. "Do they even wash here? And Inger does nothing about it?"

"She's here, so doesn't that matter?" Norm shouted.

"We have enough money to feed the globe generously and still have leftover for our parties," I retorted, blazing with anger. "It's time you were honest with yourself. We aren't doing everything we can."

"Inger is doing this for show," Pizzette mumbled from behind her hands, still reeling. "I don't feel like my presence here is going to change anything."

In a second, a screen of transparent white closed off the front of the car and the driver from the rest of us. Norm stood up despite the rocking of the car, his face set in stone. "Hold out your hands, palm facing up."

"What kind of archaic punishment is this?" Pizzette whined, obeying only because he was humongous, and we were skinny girls.

"Something from the last era," I added, dropping my fingers dramatically, saving the best for last. *I'm not scared of you people. Norm is probably a criminal like Inger too.*

Norm grabbed Pizzette's hand and jerked her smallest finger backward so fast the snap did not even register in my ears. It was only when she cried out in surprise that I realized he hurt her. He tossed her back into the seat and turned on me, his eyes shining with dark humor. "What were you saying?"

All of my bravado was gone. I trembled, sitting down obediently and folded my hands on my lap. Pizzette was swearing under her breath. I felt like joining in.

"Disobedient, privileged girls," Norm muttered, shaking his head and sitting down as if nothing had happened. "You think you're so above the rest of us."

Not anymore, but at least I knew I would never be as low as Inger Kaleon and the rest of team.

***

Pizzette

Norm eventually grew tired of listening to me sing curses and set my finger in a makeshift splint made of Luck's hair ribbon. He said it was hardly worse than a fracture. I was convinced it was never going to lie straight again.

Luck and I were silent as the car arrived at our small compound that was guarded by dogs and a flimsy fence. I could not decide which was more off-putting. We filed out onto the dead grass lawn, eager to get away from Norm.

Mattie was staring at the three buildings with a curious look on her face. She was not dressed the same as us, and it probably made her stick out more. At least my clothes were on the same level visually as the dirt.

Calling the buildings houses would have been too generous. They were shacks with sinking ceilings and clear plastic sheets flapping in the windows.

"Really?" Inger hissed, stepping in front of Mattie. "This is the best Pigladen has to offer?"

"Yes. That's the problem we're here to fix," Norm answered with an air of arrogance.

"Knock off the pride, Norm. It doesn't fit you," Lady Arabella said, walking around to Inger's other side.

The drivers carried our things inside. Inger, Lady Arabella, Norm, Petrakova, and Mattie walked into the first shack with the nicest roof, leaving Miss Jessica to claim the second for herself, brooding as usual. Luck and I did not argue and agreed to share with the bumbling Daniels. At least we would not have any more fingers snapping.

The furniture situation was worse than Danish Mansion's. The floor was dirt, doubling as a place to stand and sleep. The bathroom door rattled unpredictably, and the water that came through the faucets was a yellowish brown. I was glad I took a bottle from home, though I was not sure how to make it last several days.

Luck ended up next to me as I opened the bags of new clothes we were given. There was only one nightgown and one other dress with more suspicious polka dots. I sighed, and then zipped the bag shut and paced around the small shack. Holding onto my diamond kept me from going insane.

After some time, everyone decided the outdoors held more promise and took their boxed lunches out to the sun-bleached lawn. The people of Pigladen gathered around the gates and watched us intently. When I raised my water bottle to my lips, dozens of them reached forward. The dogs barked menacingly, and they backed up momentarily until someone else decided to hydrate themselves, restarting the cycle.

Petrakova was the only one of us that was not fazed at all. The longer I looked at her, the more familiar she seemed. If I had a full set of memories, I might have remembered what was so memorable about her face. Her presence was unnerving, since she was so young, and no other servants had showed up. Inger was in no way thrilled by us knowing each other and had never bothered to properly explain what she was doing here. Petrakova spoke with her pretty accent and carried on like everything was normal, which upset Inger even more. When she and Luck started talking, that sent her over the edge.

"Matilda, you should find something for Petrakova to do until the other servants arrive. I can't imagine why they're late."

Mattie stood up slowly, closing the lid over her uneaten food. "We can tidy up the shack a bit. Make it comfortable for the night."

"I'd prefer if you stayed outdoors. Go pull weeds." Inger pointed, and the Royal Advisor followed.

Mattie looked over her shoulder, her gaze landing on me like she wanted to say something.

My brain was trying very hard to make me remember the servant girl. "Who is she?" I mouthed.

Mattie's mouth did not move. She tapped her bare wrist twice, and then pulled Petrakova away to go weed the dead lawn. I was not sure if it was a nervous tick of hers, or if she had just told me to wait until later to find out.

***

Mattie

Isobel and I picked at weeds for three hours while the crowd stared, and Inger's group chatted. The sun was undeniably hot in this end of the country, and I was unaccustomed to the burden on the back of my neck and shoulders. Isobel kept up a nicer attitude than me, telling me stories about Marmi and the house they had and how she was going to find her soon.

"Yeah," I whispered, snapping a green blade in my hands. "I bet you're going to see her in a few days."

"I know." Isobel's eyes sparkled and she rubbed a spot on her wrist, probably where some sort of charm used to stay. "I'm glad you're going to help me."

"I am?" It dawned on me that the automatic responses I had been spitting out were sounding true to her. I had given no thought to what I was saying before letting anything slide. "I mean, of course I am. I'll be glad to do anything for you."

Isobel's smile faltered. She bent her head and kept pulling up weeds, laying them in neat piles by her knees. "Are you looking for your mother too?"

My vision blurred, a headache blooming behind my eyes. "No, Isobel. Not everyone in the world has a family."

"Mattie." I expected a hug or another one of her optimistic smiles, but instead she tapped my shoulder, compelling me to look at her.

"Yup?"

"My name is Petrakova Selle," she said slowly, her chin quivering.

"I know." I massaged my forehead, wishing for rain and cold to bring me back to Cyan City. I was no help to anyone if my headaches prevented me from seeing. "You tell everyone."

"You called me Isobel."

My heart plummeted. "I'm sorry. It was a slip of the tongue. You just look like her…the pictures that were edited. It's nothing."

"I have a family, and my own last name," Isobel said quietly, a tear rolling down her cheek. "It's Selle, not Lagarde. Don't forget who I am, Mattie. Everyone always forgets me."

I tore my eyes away from her distraught face, my head hurting worse with every breath. *You're an idiot, and now you made her cry. She doesn't want to be a princess, and she doesn't want to know who she is. She wants her mother, and you're too selfish to tell her it's too late. You want her to think you're a hero or something.*

"I'm sorry, Petrakova. It was an accident." But that was a lie. Soon, I would have to be honest with her. Judging by her reaction, she would not be thrilled. Maybe someone like me who never had anything would leap at the idea of being lost royalty, but this girl's mind was not corrupted by money and lust for power. She was only thinking about her adoptive family. Mother.

Isobel stood up and walked away from me.

"Wait." I dove forward, falling to my knees. What was wrong with me? Whatever heavy emotion I was feeling was making my head hurt and my sight spin. My balance was gone. All I could see was the princess walking toward her deranged aunt, probably to ask an innocent, clueless question. And I was stuck on the ground.

Isobel patted Inger's shoulder. My stomach was in knots as I watched the witch turn around slowly. Isobel whispered something in her ear that made Inger's eyes burn.

Then she looked at me, her mouth set in a frown.

"Sure. They're in Mattie's bag," Inger said, loud enough for me to hear. "Go inside the house. You'll see them."

I forced myself to stand up, doubled over and gasping. *One foot in front of the other. Just breathe. Breathe.* I had never had a headache like this before. None of them had ever made me feel so awful and powerless. *Sad, angry, and hopeless. A thousand other emotions I can never understand.*

For a second, I was not even in Pigladen with Inger. I was in a hospital bed, surrounded by unfamiliar faces and feeling very helpless and afraid. *We're so sorry, Mattie.*

I was wrenched from the vision and thrust back into Pigladen. Norm's bulky arms.

"What's her problem?" Lady Arabella sniffed. "She keeps fainting and falling all over the place."

"I don't know." Inger glared at me. "I'll have to ask the doctor."

Norm set me back on my feet. "She looks pale, Inger. Should I take her inside?"

Inger's voice could have killed someone. "Do you need to be the one to take that worthless girl inside? She has two legs. Let her use them."

I did, and after stumbling a couple times I made it to our cottage. The door was left ajar, so I pulled it shut behind me. "Petrakova," I called out, navigating the room in the dwindling light. "It's Mattie. I came to talk to you."

Isobel was sitting in the middle of the floor with her back to me. My bags were next to her, ransacked for a few important binders.

No. I rushed forward, grabbing her shoulder in a vain effort to stop her. "Petrakova wait…"

She was holding a crinkled picture in her hands, staring at the face with wide eyes. Eyes that mirrored the ones in the image below. But it was impossible. Everyone knew Princess Isobel Lagarde was supposed to be dead.

"I can explain," I said quickly, tearing the picture away from her. "Petrakova, this is going to be a lot to understand at once…"

"That's me?" she asked in a small voice, gesturing to the piles of documents on her family and secrets no one but Inger and I knew. "This is all about me?"

"Yes." I held her shoulders, forcing her to look in my eyes. "Please don't panic."

"Too late," she hissed, sobs engulfing her words. "Marmi is gone, right? And so is everyone else."

Cyrana. Indio. Her biological parents. "I'm so sorry, Isobel."

"And Inger...she brought me here to make sure I went where the rest of them did. It was all a lie. Since that man in the woods I thought I dreamed about, and that doctor in a white lab coat...it's been a lie. A lie I haven't been able to put together."

I nodded, too ashamed of myself.

"And..." She finally looked at me, any semblance of trust or joy gone. "You've known all along?"

"Isobel, I swear I was trying to find a way to tell you."

She batted my arms away, shaking her head. "I don't want to listen to you. I don't want you to feel sorry for me."

"You need someone to get you out of here, and that's what I'm going to do."

"I needed someone to help me find Marmi, not tell me I'm some princess." Isobel shoved me backwards. *No.* Her hands never left her side, yet I clattered to the floor, my head hitting the ground hard.

The fight was over instantly.

"Mattie? Mattie!"

I had no idea how she had done it, but suddenly I had a word for my emotions. They were all too overwhelming now.

Despair, Mattie. All this sadness is called despair.

***

Pizzette

Dinner was a quiet affair on the lawn. We opened boxes of cold meats and bread and ate them with the Pigladen crowd watching us. Twenty minutes in, Luck excused herself and went back inside, leaving the box for the Daniels to split. "Can I go inside too?" I asked.

After Norm's assault and Mattie's weird fainting spell, I was ready to run while they were distracted. My life was of more value to me than whatever fake diplomatic show Inger was putting on. All she had done so far was sit on the lawn and eat.

"Fine. Be ready tomorrow for work. By tomorrow, I mean midnight."

I pressed my knuckles into my cheeks. "My, that's a quick turnaround."

Norm gave me one disapproving look. I shut up and went inside to find Luck who was using my bag as a chair and brushing her hair. She waved without turning to look at me.

"I have to be honest." I walked around and sat in front of her, drawing my knees up to my chin. "This place is making me wish I was in Cyan. That says a lot."

"We're actually going to die," Luck murmured, yanking the brush through a tangle. "Inger is a murderer."

"That wouldn't surprise me, seeing who she surrounds herself with."

"Cordelia. That was all Inger's fault." Luck started tying another ribbon around her curls. "It was almost mine."

She's being serious.

"Then why on Earth are you here? You should be with the police." Her calmness was never going to make sense to me, but what have I been doing really, sitting with own information and keeping my mouth shut out of fear? I did not know there was another person in this country that was as wary of Inger as I was.

"They wouldn't do a thing. Inger pays them hush money probably." Luck inhaled slowly, staring at her feet for a moment. "I thought I could figure out her game, but it's too hard. I can't go snooping in the main house with everyone watching, and she probably has a sniper hiding somewhere." She pulled her dress down over her knees, pointing at the polka dots with shaking fingers. "Don't the dots line up strange? Over my kneecaps and right under my ribs. A couple on my back, slightly more on the left than right. In the dark they're still so bright."

I shook my head. "I think it's an ugly print."

Luck laughed, but her face was absent of a smile. "This is why I skip grade levels and you barely make it."

"Wow, that's really nice of you to point out."

"They're targets, Pizzette. Inger wants to kill me because she knows what I saw and you…" She rolled her eyes, rubbing the tip of the ribbon against her lips. "You're the Sneak, right? She finally cornered you."

"Is it obvious? Here I was thinking us winning this trip was a nasty convenience, especially right after we found out our parents were having an affair with each other."

"Ha. That really made my holiday special."

It was clear Luck disliked me, and I was not too fond of her, but we were trapped here. "Luck, we need to leave. Inger wants to start this diplomatic nonsense tomorrow, and if your theory is correct…we aren't safe."

"I thought you figured that out when Norm almost broke your finger. Cyan is led by insane people, Pizzette. I think we need to find someone on the outside to help us. I know the world nations barely tolerate each other after World War Four to maintain peace, but Cyan is going to fall apart. Enter extreme martial law. We can't let that happen."

I stood up, grabbing her hand. "Then let's make for the doors and sprint back to the city. I'm sure no one will stop us."

"Stop being sarcastic and stupid," Luck huffed, slapping my wrist. "We are going to wait until Inger's about to strike, then fight back. Break away long enough to hijack one of those cars and get out of here."

"You're going to fight back against people like the Daniels?"

"Yes."

"*Norm?*"

"Yeah…" Luck scratched behind her ear, pursing her lips. "Maybe the dogs can help us. They seem aggressive."

"They are, and they are going to attack us too if they're set loose."

"That's why I didn't finish my dinner you idiot, so we'd have bait to use on them."

"The Daniels took care of it for you." I crossed my arms. Luck did the same, just as annoyed as I was. "Accept that we don't have a plan other than to be squashed by Inger."

"What about that girl? Lady Matilda?"

"She's one of Inger's advisors, star student. I wouldn't trust her with our lives yet." She gave me what seemed like a clue earlier on but had not followed up on it. I was too desperate to keep waiting.

"I'm banking on you, and the servant," Luck snapped.

"That girl can't be older than seven or eight. What can she do?"

"More than the advisor, according to your logic."

"Maybe I can contact Clint from the palace. Tomas."

"Are your guard friends teleporters? I don't see how they'll get here by midnight, or what phone you're going to use to call them."

I had never had a sister to bicker with but trying to reason with Luck was giving me an idea. "Stop denouncing everything I'm saying when your plans aren't much better."

"Stop saying things that are illogical if you don't want them to be denounced."

Both of us stopped arguing when someone knocked on the door.

"Great. Inger came early," I muttered under my breath, wondering which of the four bags in the room I could hide behind.

"You want to answer?" Luck mumbled, stomping me over to the door by my arm. "Go on. I think she likes you more."

"You'd really give me up that fast?"

"Plan B; you're the distraction." Luck pulled open the door, and Inger Kaleon was not waiting for us.

Instead, it was our little friend Petrakova. She looked like she had been crying.

"I need your help," she said in a grave voice. "I made Mattie fall and hit her head and now she isn't waking up."

***

Luck

Petrakova led us through the dark, skirting around the campfire Inger's crowd surrounded, while keeping her voice low. Her story did not make sense until we were inside Inger's cottage, right in the middle of the crime scene.

Amid a mess of wrinkled paper and files was Mattie, out cold with her arms by her sides and hair covering half of her face. There was a growing bruise on her forehead, stark against her even skin tone. I whirled around, my eyes meeting Pizzette's. She looked as cautious as I felt, hovering near the back in case Petrakova pulled a knife on us. Had she really pushed Mattie?

"Did you check her vitals?" I asked quietly, prodding Petrakova's shoulders. "What happened? She's bigger than you, and that looks serious."

Petrakova scrubbed her eyes with the back of her hand, still looking determined as she knelt next to Mattie and dropped her wrist across her knees. She pressed her fingers against Mattie's arm, nodding to herself. "I can feel it."

"Do you want to move her somewhere comfortable?" Pizzette offered.

I scowled at her. "Look around and find me something comfortable."

She shrugged, taking a few steps forward and squatting next to Mattie. It felt weird and invasive for all of us to be standing over her while she was gone to the world, surveying her like an experiment.

"Petrakova, you have to tell us what happened," I said as nicely as I could, placing my hand on her shoulder. She was fixating too hard on Mattie's still face, as if to commit it to memory.

Petrakova shook her head. "Mattie needs an ice pack."

"Right, let me just reach behind me and find one." I bit my lip, instantly wishing I had not spoken with such a harsh tone. Petrakova barely reacted.

Pizzette moved Mattie off the notebooks, her arm falling away from Petrakova. "Luck, help me move her to that pallet."

Inger had a pallet in her room? I groaned, wrapping my hands around Mattie's skinny ankles and straining to pick her up. We carried her over to the corner and laid her on the bed, still feeling like it was not enough.

"Should we tell Inger?" Pizzette asked. "Or is this when we run?"

Petrakova tried to wriggle around us, but I grabbed her arm. Out of all the criminals here, I would never believe she was one. "I'm giving you one chance to explain yourself. I know you're a kid, but you're smart. None of this innocent act matters when someone gets hurt, especially if it had something to do with you."

"Luck," Pizzette hissed, going back to the papers on the floor. "Look at this."

"After Petrakova answers me." I stared at the little girl, pity filling me quickly. She had stopped crying, but those emotionless brown eyes were scarier than any expression Inger let out. "Come on."

"This is important. Like…it changes everything."

"Pizzette, give us a minute." I took a deep breath, praying Inger would not open the door and find us here. It was getting late. The Daniels would go inside soon and find us missing. We would be exposed in seconds, and then maybe the polka dot dresses would be put to good use a little earlier than planned.

"She already figured it out," Petrakova whispered, nodding her head toward Pizzette. "Mattie was trying to tell me, and then…she flew."

"Right." I let go of her and walked over to Pizzette's side. "What are you looking at?"

Pizzette shoved a picture into my hands, still skimming over the papers and silently mouthing the words. It took me half a second to identify the face.

"It's Petrakova. So?"

"Read the back."

I flipped it over, the air suddenly a thousand times staler.

Princess Isobel Garnet Lagarde; prediction for age seven to nine years.

Petrakova came and stood behind us, her voice trembling. "Everyone here knows now. Inger is going to make sure we never leave."

"We have to get out of here," I said under my breath. "Now. Forget the dogs and the dresses. I'm running scared."

"Wait." Pizzette was still gripping the papers tightly, her eyes flooding with tears. "It looks like Mattie wrote this. Inger has a plan to dispose of all of us because…oh my God."

"What is it?" I leaned over, trying to tamp down my own hysteria.

The girl with the diamond necklace, Pizzette, got it from someone else. Inger searched the system. That man's name was Palmer Colfer, the same man in the video who rescued Isobel and died in the Burning. The girl most likely has no idea.

I had never even thought to ask where her father was. I had been so wrapped up in being mad at Papa that it had never occurred to me. He did not just leave his family one day.

Pizzette did not have a father. Not anymore. Maybe not ever.

"Pizzette…" I was at a loss for words. "I'm so sorry."

Pizzette crushed the diamond between her hands and sobbed, her cries echoing in my head.

I had never thought a diplomatic observation trip would turn into this.

"Let's go." I stood up on shivering legs, my pulse racing. "We can wake up Mattie—"

The doorknob jiggled, and half a second later, the door opened.

***

Mattie

I opened my eyes slowly to a throbbing headache, the world dark and blurry around me. Muffled voices made their way into my brain, but I could not understand what they meant. Through slanted vision, I saw Inger cross the cottage in two steps, seize Isobel's arm, and shove her against the wall.

No. I reached forward, falling off the pallet and onto my face. "Inger, let go of her."

Inger turned her gaze on me, her smoldering eyes stopping me. "We don't have to draw this out any longer."

I pushed myself off the floor, scanning the room for anything I could fight her with. Escape. We needed to escape.

Out of the corner of my eye, I saw two shadows slinking toward the door, previously huddled behind a stack of boxes. *Pizzette and Luck?*

"She doesn't have to be your enemy," I said feebly. Isobel struggled against Inger, but her hold was strong. She looked at me for help.

"You know that is a lie. I have many enemies."

"I won't make any more Preserv if you hurt her," I challenged, pretending I was at an advantage and not crumpled on the floor.

"I could threaten you too," Inger snapped.

"With what? You know I have nobody I care about." Pizzette and Luck made it out the door, barely replacing it before Inger continued her rant.

"Lying again. Who's that guard Arabella saw you with? Tomas? I can kill him too."

My face burned. *Not Tomas.*

"You wouldn't dare." My voice was impossibly small.

"Stop acting brave." Inger smirked, dropping Isobel on the floor and sauntering over to me. She grabbed my chin, forcing my head up so her eyes were inches from mine. "You were never bold."

"I don't know what your game is, but you won't win," I hissed.

"Isn't it obvious?" Inger asked in a mocking voice. "I thought I made myself pretty clear."

"One day everyone is going to know what you did," I spat. "And they will never call you queen."

The fake smile dropped. Inger's fingers tightened, cutting off my air for a second.

I kneed her in the stomach, her grip loosening.

"Isobel, run!"

Inger glanced over her shoulder. The girl was smarter than the both of us and had already sprinted for the door.

"You will stop where you stand," Inger ordered her. "Or I break this girl's neck."

Isobel froze with her hand on the doorknob, her wide eyes shimmering.

"Just go," I coughed. "I don't care." *I don't care...who doesn't care about their own life?*

Isobel shook her head, and then closed the door. Backed away from it.

"That's a good girl," Inger crowed. "Now sit down and behave. When I'm done with Mattie, I will address you."

Isobel sat on the floor next to my bag, staring right past Inger at me. "Get ready."

"What?" Inger's eyes floated between us, confused.

It took all of three seconds for the yelling to start. Two for the door to come crashing down.

One before an enormous black guard dog ran into the cottage. Straight toward Inger.

***

Pizzette

The papers were burning a hole in my shoulder where my camisole strap pinned them in place. Next to me, Luck was shaking and asking me if I was sure for the tenth time.

"We need to get Mattie and Isobel out of that house and distract everyone else," I said, wiping the last tear from my face.

"But those things aren't human. They won't understand who to attack. I wasn't being completely serious when I suggested it." Luck followed me over to where the dogs were tied up. Two mutts and a pit bull that made me wish I had overslept this morning growled at us from the other side of the gate where the crowd had finally disappeared.

"Well Inger might be slow, and Mattie and Isobel could be faster." *Isobel. That girl is the princess.* I was hardly ever responsible for myself, but now many lives depended on what I did in the next few minutes. "I'll run in behind the dogs, and you start the second diversion."

"A second one?" Her voice cracked as I undid one of the knots.

"Start up one of the cars and make it look like you're about to drive away. I trust you know how to do that at least. Wait for the three of us to leave the cottage, and then we'll run." Another knot came loose. One of the dogs nearly jumped over the fence. Luck screamed out loud.

It did not matter. The last knot came undone, and the beasts broke through their enclosure and into the compound.

One of them ran right across me, its back leg whacking me in the face. The other two followed, attracted to the dinner being shared over the fire.

"Go," I yelled to Luck, and then pushed her when she did not move fast enough.

I sprinted toward Inger's cottage, my eyes only on the door. There was no hidden guard to help me now. I had to be my own hero.

Rough arms grabbed me around the waist, pulling me off the ground and away from my destination. *Norm.*

"What the hell are you girls planning?" he griped in my ear.

"Call it revenge." I drove my heel into his leg, throwing my full body weight forward. We both fell to the ground, and I was quick to wriggle away before he caught me again.

Everyone was shouting, the dogs creating more panic than I anticipated. Lady Arabella squealed, shielding her face while Mr. Daniels pulled a knife on one of the dogs. The champ easily disarmed him.

"Good boy," I murmured, continuing toward the house. One of the dogs had found its way inside, and the scene was not pretty.

Inger was swinging at it with her knife, swearing and yelling for Norm. Mattie was still in her grip, a shield blocking her from the snapping beast. She saw me and looked like she was about to cry.

"Isobel," Inger roared, finally throwing Mattie to the side so she could stop her. I ran, intent on tackling the witch. *The Burning. She started it. She killed my father.*

The paper was a confession in someone else's writing. This monster would never be able to say it.

"Leave her alone," I cried, shoving Inger to the floor. The dog jumped on my back, catching a tangle of my hair in its mouth.

Mattie was screaming behind me, trying to pull it off. "Let go."

Inger righted herself, pointing the knife at me. "You first."

Isobel intercepted her strike, swinging a bag into Inger's arm. The knife clattered to the floor, it's pearly handle reflecting light from the campfire. Fire. *Everything is burning.*

I looked around, terrified. The flames surrounded my body, encasing me in a smoky coffin while the heat choked me. There was no escape. The doors had turned to ash long ago and the ceiling would not hold…it was going to come crashing down soon with me underneath, pinned under a massive coffin of fire.

I tried to scream, but nothing would come. My body was immobile, and I was trapped…

I heard Isobel grunt, and then a heavy thud. Inger falling to the floor. The regular, dirt floor.

The flames had disappeared, as if they had never been there in the first place.

Isobel put her hand on the dog's back, whispering something under her breath. As if under control, the animal released my hair and stalked over to the corner where it sat waiting obediently.

"Did you see that?" I asked in a haggard voice, lightly touching the back of my head. There was a spot that was already swollen and sticky, but at least I was still alive. In one piece. "The fire?"

"There was nothing." Isobel offered me a hand. "Where is Luck? Is this the escape plan?"

"Outside, and yeah, we're putting it together as we go." I winced, rubbing my head. Was I losing it? "Are you sure you guys didn't see anything? It felt so real."

"Never mind that. Isobel, what did you do to Inger?" Mattie asked as we made for the door, breathless.

"I slapped her face."

"But she's so much bigger than you…" Mattie stopped talking once we got outside.

Oh my…

The Daniels were waiting, armed to the teeth. Norm and Lady Arabella were off by the fences, a second barrier blocking us. Somewhere, Miss Jessica was probably sulking, waiting for her cue.

"Don't be stupid," Mr. Daniels said with a smirk. "We wouldn't want our diplomatic observation to end early, right?"

"Isobel, stand behind us," I whispered, raising my arms slowly.

"Wait." She pointed across the compound, the Daniels' eyes following. "Our ride's here."

One of the cars crashed through the gate. Luck was screaming behind the wheel, crushing the pedal as she barreled toward us.

Everyone with their grip on reality dove out of the way as the vehicle crashed into Miss Jessica's cottage.

We wasted no time. Luck threw open the door and nearly fell out, the car's engine still running.

"Get up. I hate this place," Luck coughed, fanning her face. "I'm going to be sick, oh my gosh…"

We ran toward the fence and hopped over. There was shouting behind us, drowned out by the sounds of dogs yapping and the townspeople calling out.

"Where are we going?" Luck gasped, pushing ahead of the rest of us.

"Lead the way, Lucky Star," I grumbled.

"Cyan. We have to get back to Cyan before Inger," Mattie explained for us.

We merged into the streets, taking several turns to confuse our pursuers. We were on some wayward path to the river. "We have the true princess of Cyan with us now, and Inger will kill us on sight."

In the dark, Isobel almost blended in with the shadows, but her presence was unmistakable. Rumors or not, the princess of Cyan was alive, and at the moment only had the three of us working to keep her alive.

***

Part 5

Luck

Crossing Mudlark Moat two hours after midnight was not as easy as Mattie made it sound. She never explicitly said it would not be a challenge, but the confidence she had while waving us in the direction of the gates was misleading. Every step sent me sinking into holes filled with mud. I slipped, no longer so graceful once one of my shoes came off.

"Careful, Lady Luck," Pizzette muttered, laughing to herself. "You might go missing in one of those."

"I don't hike through mountains and bushes frequently." I lifted my skirt up over my knees, grimacing at how dirty I had become just within a few hours. "There are so many flies. I don't think I've ever seen a creature with more than two legs or wings in the city."

"Everything dies in Cyan. You probably blinked and missed it altogether." Pizzette extended her arms out like a cross, pretending to walk on a tightrope around two exceptionally large holes.

Her aloofness was starting to rub me the wrong way. "You were there for a month, and you spent that month inside school. You saw none of this city, and even less of this country."

"Actually, I used to live here." Pizzette fell off her toes, barely regaining her balance before hitting the ground. "I don't remember much of it, but I've been here before."

I clapped my hands. "Wonderful. You're completely brilliant."

Pizzette stuck out her tongue. "Smarter than you."

"No."

"Whose idea was it to set the dogs free?"

I was about to yell something in reply when Mattie stepped between us, looking like a mountain made out of misery. "I have an idea. Both of you be quiet so no one finds us before we make it back to the city."

"I'm hoping someone finds me," I whispered, stomping ahead of her. "I wasn't meant to end up shoeless in a dried-up river with Diamond Freak."

I saw Pizzette's face fall, even in the dark. I considered taking back my words, but Mattie's scolding interrupted me.

"The princess of Cyan is with us. Can't you pull yourselves together and realize how important this is? A miracle occurred, and you're both bitter about some silly competition."

Pizzette and I were quiet. I willed Mattie to shut up, but she kept talking.

"This is larger than our lives. Isobel restoring the Lagarde line means order will be maintained. There won't be mass panic or protests when Inger tries to take the throne, and the family bestowed with the Regal Gift will continue to rule."

"You sure know a lot," I grumbled, scratching a bug bite on my arm.

"I studied under Inger for about eight years." Mattie's eyes widened as she quickly tried to correct herself. "Not that I'm trying to support her. I simply…"

I faced her, all my patience gone. "What did you do in the palace for eight years? How do we know you aren't about to lead us to one of her secret houses?"

Mattie shook her head, taking a few steps back toward Pizzette. "I mean every word when I say I despise Inger Kaleon and wish she had never taken me from the hospital."

I wrinkled my nose. "Hospital? She didn't adopt you from your birth mother or anything, right?"

Mattie shook her head again, even more frenetically. "No. I've been an orphan for as long as I can remember. I fell ill, and she happened to be passing through the town when I was admitted to the hospital."

I glanced at Pizzette and Isobel, wondering if Mattie's story seemed good enough to them. Pizzette had gone back to circling the holes like a child, and Isobel's eyes had not left the ground. My consulting party was useless.

"Well how long have you known about Isobel? You probably knew Inger was going to kill us too."

Mattie tripped and fell on her backside, splattering mud everywhere. It was a pitiful display.

"I'm stuck, Luck. In case you haven't noticed, there's no one in Cyan to depend on when the assumed queen turns out to be a murderer. What was I supposed to do? Take my story to Gallen? Catch the midnight train? Inger is always watching me. I never had the chance to leave." Mattie swiped her hand across her face, sniffling. "But I was going to tonight, even if it put me on Inger's bad side. I have the DNA tests and plenty of evidence in my lab at the palace. I just needed an opportunity to get away from her."

"I'm glad we're you're opportunity," Pizzette chimed in. "My month wasn't wasted. I have evidence of my own as well."

I gawked at her. "You really are a Sneak."

"Not really. The papers were on the floor in front of everyone." She pulled a wad of papers out of her dress, flattening them out like we could read it in the moonlight. "Isobel's pictures and notes Mattie wrote about Inger's plans. I think this, combined with some DNA evidence and the actual princess, we can convince anyone of the truth."

We all looked at Isobel again, worried about her silence. She had been so happy and determined a few hours ago. I did not remember the giggling girl I met in the hallway.

"Isobel, can you talk to us?" Mattie whispered. I held out my hand and pulled her up from the mud.

"I'm sorry for pushing you. You have a bump."

Mattie's fingers brushed against her temple like she hadn't noticed the bruise. "It's okay. I think a good knock in the head helps the mind."

Isobel lifted her eyes. Tears were clinging to her lashes. "I'm always going to be lonely," she whispered, her voice crumbling.

"What?" Pizzette knelt in front of her, grabbing Isobel's face and staring into her eyes. "That's not true, and you know what? You're never going to be alone because you have the three of us."

"She won't be alone. She'll have all of Cyan," I said, crossing my arms.

"That's not what she means, Luck," Mattie whispered.

"Did you hear me?" Pizzette asked the princess, smiling. "We'll be your friends."

Isobel nodded, and then slid her arms around Pizzette.

Great. I pinched my arm to stop myself from feeling silly and emotional. We could all talk about being friends later. We were still out in the open, and Inger could send every officer in the country after us. She probably had at this point.

"We'll be too slow if we walk the whole time," I said to Mattie. "You mentioned the midnight train?"

She shrugged. "That's just a saying."

"It's real life. Not a train, but a bus." I scanned the shadowy horizon, the quiet of the woods and gone river confirming what I dreaded. "How close do you think the nearest stop is, and how fast can a bus get us to Cyan?"

***

"This is a disaster." Miscellanea Daniels rubbed her hands on her pants, smearing the mud already staining them. Outside the shack, the crowds were shouting again, their midnight display too arousing for the small town. The dogs Norm had managed to tie up were grumpy, adding to the noise with their impatient barks as he dug through the storage bins for food. Somehow, he was in the best position out of everyone in the group. At least he did not have to face Inger.

"No, I thought this was perfectly optimal," Arabella drawled, crossing her arms. "They were sneaking through your shack. You and your husband are supposed to be good at trapping people. How did they escape your locks?"

Miscellaneous Daniels shrugged, and then looked at his wife. "The locks?"

Arabella's nostrils flared. "Don't you remember the Burning, and the fancy locks you put on the main doors? It took tens of guards to break them."

"Oh." Miss Daniels pursed her lips. "Those...we might have brought the wrong set."

Mr. Daniels frowned. "Or forgotten them altogether."

Arabella glared at them for a minute and threw up her hands. "Inger, you deal with these idiots."

Miss Daniels quickly pointed at Miss Jessica, who had been hunched over a cell phone for the last hour. "She didn't do anything to restrain them. She watched them run away with the rest of us."

"I'm contacting my daughter," Jessica growled, her dark hair hiding her face. "She's trying to access the cameras along the route to the city. The girls must have taken the most direct path back."

"We should be on the road looking for them. They have the princess," Mr. Daniels said.

Inger and Arabella had been talking quietly in the corner. They both looked up at him with murder in their eyes. *Shut up.*

"Lucienne cut the power in the other two vehicles. Disabled the batteries by splicing a few wires," Arabella said through tight teeth. "The stupid clever girl outsmarted us."

"We have to rent one from this town."

"A horse and buggy, you mean? Nothing here is fast enough." Inger sighed, punching the wall with her fist. "I'm having something brought in from the Moatside Villages, but it will take time. The girls will be far ahead of us."

"Then we'll never catch them," Mr. Daniels snapped. "We've already lost."

"Don't be so short-sighted." Arabella stepped forward, lifting her sharp chin. "We have a backup plan for when everything else fails."

Miss Daniels lifted her brow. "We do?"

Jessica snorted, still focused on her conversation. "Ida found them. They've boarded public transport at the edge of the river leading into one of the villages."

"They'll be in Cyan even faster," Miss Daniels whined. "They'll expose us. Our lives are over."

"Mattie will go to her lab for evidence, and that bumbling crew will try to make it to the Radio Tower on the south end of the city which broadcasts all the way to Towering Heights and some parts of Gallen. They will spout their story and reveal that they have found the princess," Inger summarized in a bored voice.

"*Yes*," the Daniels moaned. "How can you be so calm when everything we have been planning for so long has completely fallen to pieces?"

"Because they will never make it that far. I have the guards and police on my side. When Jessica is finished, I will phone the palace and ask them to detain the girls until we arrive. No need to sweat. We'll arrive just in time for the show."

***

Pizzette

Though I did not complain like Luck, I was grateful to be out of the mud and on a heated bus back to the city.

Four young girls walking along a dry riverbed in the early hours of the morning was too rare a sight. All three of the passengers taking their joy ride stared at us while we sat down in two rows of cushioned seats. I made sure Isobel's hood was back over her head, and that she was closest to the blacked-out windows. Her little feet did not touch the ground.

"Have you ever ridden public transport, Luck?" I heard Mattie ask behind us.

"Do I look like someone who takes public transport?"

"You take taxis," I pointed out. "Does that count?"

"Pizzette, you should learn to shut up."

"Guys. Please." Mattie blew out a breath, pulling her muddy feet off the ground and onto her seat. "Try to rest for a few minutes. I'll keep watch."

"For what?" Luck yawned. "Like they're going to land on the roof of the bus and carry us away?"

Mattie did not respond. A few seconds later, Luck turned away and almost immediately fell asleep. I swiveled around in my seat.

"Pizzette, you know about your father, right?" Mattie whispered.

Yes. All my life, I had wondered what had happened to him and why my memory always seemed fragmented. Finding out tonight did not have the magical, earth-shattering healing power I had hoped it would. Instead, I felt emptier than ever.

I nodded, picking at my nails and avoiding her eyes. "Next question?"

"I'm sure you are feeling a lot of despair right now," she said in her pointed voice, still pinning me with her eyes. "And want to cry but are trying not to because you're not sure if it'll make a difference."

"Wow, you're so perceptive."

"I am. I've always tried to fill the holes in my own memory by learning from others. Copying their behavior so I don't feel so out of place." Mattie rested her chin on her hands, looking somewhere past me. "I'm not good at figuring out what I'm feeling all the time, but I can see it in others. You're missing the life you've forgotten. The one where you had him."

"Wrong." I blinked quickly, pressing the diamond against my cheek. "I don't even remember it."

"You're missing the idea of having a father because you know that he is truly gone. You've been hanging onto the mystery, always wondering where he was. But you know now, and you don't want to stop searching for him."

I sniffled, pinching my arm to stop myself from crying. "Mattie, I'm fine. I don't want to talk right now."

"Do not despair," she whispered, touching my arm. "He loved his family. The sacrifice he made that day was for the future of this country, his daughter's home." Mattie tried to smile. "I know you miss him. It's okay to stop joking. There's no one you need to hide from."

"Yeah, yeah." I sniffled again, and then wiped my nose with my sleeve. The diamond was glimmering in the moonlight, still present though I finally found out the truth about the owner. "I guess he isn't gone yet. I still have his diamond."

Mattie nodded, and then glanced at Isobel. The princess was fogging up the glass with her breath and then tracing little figures in the fog. She was more emotionally sound than Mattie and me.

"Go to sleep for a bit," Mattie said. "I'll wake you up when we get there."

"Okay." I rested my head back, trying to remember what it felt like to be oblivious and young. Content with doodling on a car window while Mom and I drove to the marketplace. Overjoyed at the simple thought of having extra dessert or sweets after dinner. Still hanging onto the hope that the previous owner of my necklace would come walking through the door one night, holding out his arms to both of us and admitting he had only been lost, but had searched for us for so long…

My eyes closed, and a slew of nightmares took me away to sleep.

***

Mattie

I was the only one awake after two hours of quiet. Other passengers had come and gone, off to work in the mines or the trash and recycling plants scattered around the Moatside Villages. The driver was still skeptical, but I stood up twice and walked to the front to remind him we knew our destination was the city, and that we had some way to pay. Of course, *I* did not, but my rich companions would be able to cover it.

Yawning, I stretched my legs into the aisle, swirling my stained boots in the air and whistling. I longed for one of my books or journals to lose myself in. Being here with other people who were friendly was making me miss the idea of a family even more. When Luck had pressured me into admitting how I came to know Inger, I felt even more of that despair build up inside me. For so long, I simply pushed the idea of having anyone out of my head, so I did not have to feel anything. First, Tomas made me feel nice, and now these three were something like friends. Companions. Somehow, we had all ended up on the same line of fate, on route to the city that doomed us all but always called us back.

Cyan. Inger told me the hospital was not far from Pigladen, and that she did not know where my parents were from. I did not have Cyan pale skin and straight hair. My eyes, though blue, were brighter, my skin dark and naturally speckled with freckles. There was a larger spot, directly under my left ear, that served as my only identifying mark, a birthmark Inger said the orphanage could never find anyone to recognize me by.

I remembered walking out of the hospital with her, my first caregiver in all the years of my life. She had given me an elementary reader and two notepads to scribble on, and I carried them under my arm while she talked to me under her breath.

"You'll be staying in the palace with me once reconstruction is finished. You'll have a room, a place to study and read. I gathered from your files that you excel in math and science?"

I nodded, touching the tip of a pen to my chin.

"I have work for you to do. People might think I'm crazy, but I think you can be the one to figure this out for me. Eventually."

Eventually.

In that moment, Inger could have been my friend. I had been hoping, thinking that this would be a turning point in my life. A place to start new memories and build a home.

Eventually, maybe that's what this could be.

Alone. I had always been alone in Cyan, and after this was over, maybe that would change.

Home. Maybe with Inger gone, you can finally find a place to call home.

***

Tomas hated rotations this early in the morning, especially when the school was empty, and Inger was not even at the palace. Home was waiting for him, but he bore it with gritted teeth, watching the city from a distance while leaning against the gates of the compound. No one else said a word all evening, and the silence was starting to weigh on him. Finally, when Bonne came running up behind them was there hope for conversation.

"What is it?" Clint snapped, tucking his hands into the sleeves of his new coat.

"Madame Inger just called. She said…" Bonne's face reddened, and he dropped his head. "It didn't make any sense. I swear, this woman's gone mad."

"What did she say?" Clint's patience was gone. Tomas backed away from him without thinking. A confrontation on the front lawn was not about to include him.

"She said that these girls are going to come to the palace soon, and that they will try everything they can to convince us of this ridiculous story…Never mind. I doubt it's real."

"For the sake of the rising sun, can you explain yourself?"

"Fine." Bonne looked up at them, shaking his head. "She told me two students from the school who went on the diplomatic observation tour with her, Pizzette and Lucienne, are with her Royal Advisor Matilda, and they have a little girl among them, one who bears an unmistakable resemblance to Cyrana Lagarde's lost daughter. Inger made me swear we would detain them, and make sure they were still restrained when she and her team arrive. They are planning a coup and will use the little girl to trick the world into thinking Inger is a monster."

Mattie. Tomas's feet stalled. His gasp was covered up by Clint's questions.

"Why would a group of teenage girls be planning a coup? Have you seen the lookalike? How do we know they aren't telling the truth?"

"Because Princess Isobel is dead. It has been confirmed time and time again." Bonne straightened his back, his momentary weakness gone. "We have to protect our future monarch. If this group wants to cause trouble in our peaceful city, then we have to stop them."

"I doubt their intent is to hurt anyone," Tomas said quickly, his heart racing. "I know all of them, and they are very kind."

"Are you going to help them?" Bonne raised his gun, aiming it at Tomas. "Are you in on their game? I've seen you talking to them before."

"No, I'm not helping them with anything, I just don't think Inger is making the right call," Tomas cried, refusing to draw his weapon. "You know what Inger can do to prisoners. You know she is going to do more than hurt them."

"Your job is to follow orders, not ask questions." Bonne fired a shot.

Clint jumped between them, shoving Tomas back against the gate. The bullet scraped his shoulder, missing Tomas by mere centimeters.

Bonne's face darkened. "Come on, Clint. Are you trying to get me fired? I'm doing my job. The world doesn't need another war."

"You can't have such diminished morale," Clint said carefully, holding up his hands harmlessly. "Tomas is a kid. He's still learning how to take orders."

"We could easily replace him. No one around here needs a soft-hearted guard for protection. This world isn't the same anymore. You and I both know sanity left when the world decided to go to war for the fourth time." Bonne kept his gun pointed at them, eyes on Tomas plastered against the gate. "I have ancestors in my family who served. People who died because people wouldn't listen and do what they were told. When everyone has a say, there's nothing like order anymore. Cyan is perfectly fine. We're doing fine on our own."

Clint shook his head, slowly walking toward Bonne. "It was people like you who almost ran this world to ruin, and are going to do it again, over and over. It's an endless cycle of lying and refusing to agree that everything is always going to change." He extended one hand, snow melting in his open palm. "Give me the gun and go back inside. I'll talk to Tomas."

"Complacency and obedience need to be taught in school," Bonne muttered. "This kid still thinks he has a right to do anything he wants."

"He's breaking protocol for reasonable concerns. We aren't a bunch of mindless soldiers."

"We swear to protect this palace and our leader."

"As I remember it, we take an oath to protect the crown, and if there's a chance the true heir still exists, then we shouldn't pass it up."

Tomas was frozen in place, his eyes darting between them.

"Bonne, it's time you left the palace."

A strong gust of wind blew. Bonne teetered and fell, the gun flying up in the air. Clint caught it and smacked Bonne across the face twice.

Tomas was paralyzed, frozen to the gate while watching Clint. The guard calmly took his gun, turning to Tomas.

"He's knocked out, kid. Don't look at me like that." Clint dragged Bonne to the side and leaned him against the gate. "What a despicable man. He's the type Inger likes to have around."

Tomas was still silent.

"You know I'm not going to turn them over to Inger, right?" Clint returned to his position at the gate, folding his arms with a groan. "I was trying to get through to him, but it didn't work."

"You…you saved me," Tomas sputtered, his eyes blurring. "Bonne was going to kill me."

"I was doing my job. Guarding. Now get back in line. We can't make a scene."

Tomas hurried back to his spot, adjusting his uniform and trying to fix his hair. "Thank you."

"You're too sentimental. I just jumped in the way."

"But you did it so fast, and it's not like you had any obligation to protect me."

"I did it because I'm human. I won't stand by and let something like that happen. I'm not afraid to put myself in danger for others anymore."

"Okay." Tomas closed his eyes, taking a deep breath. "I hope they're alright. The girls."

"Leave it to them to find lost treasure," Clint murmured. "I wouldn't put it past them."

Tomas turned to him, his hat lopsided. "Do you truly believe they found the princess?"

Clint nodded. "Does that make me insane?"

"No. No, I believe it too." Tomas turned back to the city, rain beginning to spot his view. "I just always had a feeling."

***

Luck

The bus stopped at the edge of the city close to the slums. Stopping after hours of steady driving jolted me awake. I yelped, nearly hitting Mattie in the face.

"Relax, Lucky Star. We're here," Pizzette said with a smirk, nudging Isobel's shoulder to wake her.

"Shut up, Diamond Freak. I panicked when I saw you and thought I was on Mars."

Pizzette was about to fire something back when Isobel giggled. Both of us looked at her.

"Mars," she said to herself. "That's funny."

Mattie glanced and shrugged. She reached for Isobel's hand, speaking in a soft voice. "We're almost at your new home."

Isobel took her hand and stood up, her hood flopping back off her head. We walked down the center aisle of the bus like a band of thugs, taking cryptic looks out the windows while Pizzette spun in a full circle behind us, checking every empty row for pursuers.

The driver stopped our charade. "The ride is two-thousand cizotes for each of you."

I gawked. "What kind of bus fare is this?"

"Nighttime fare. I don't like to drive in the dark, so I multiply the price by a couple hundred for you scraggly travelers trying to find a new place to be homeless. I'll help out by emptying your digital bank accounts."

"That's unfair. How can you expect us to cough up that much money?" Pizzette cried. "Your sign clearly shows a price of less than ten cizotes for every hour of travel."

"I don't change it with time. You girls should have noticed that no one stays on for long on the bus." The driver laughed, sliding a handheld register toward us. "Go on, enter your account name. This is my favorite part."

"Do you know who we are?" I snapped, leaning in his face. "You can't scam people like us."

Mattie pulled me back. "No, he does not know who we are, and it's probably better that way."

"You'll find a way to pay, or I'll take you to the trash yards to work it off," the driver sneered.

"You're such a prick," Pizzette growled.

He stood up. All four of us retreated back into the aisle.

"I can call the police. They love me."

I was frustrated, not because I could not afford the ride, but because he was getting away with scamming us.

"Fine," I said. "Let me enter my account information. You'll be receiving an explicit letter from my papa soon."

"Ha. I bet it'll be written on the underside of a cardboard box."

Isobel put her hand on my arm, stopping me. "Wait."

"Hey, what are you doing?" I hissed.

"I have an emergency bank account," Isobel whispered, her fingers flying over the keyboard. "Marmi gave me the password a long time ago."

Account name: Nolatore. Password: RGLaceIC.

We all stared in amazement as a profile popped up on the screen, one worth over a billion cizotes.

The driver snorted, laughing to cover up his doubt. "Is this a prank? Are you guys hackers?"

Isobel shook her head. "Marmi told me this was an account I could use. No one else owns it."

"Yeah, because the Nolatores are dead." The driver accepted the payment anyway, and then grabbed Isobel's arm, yanking her away from us. "Who are you? How do you have access to a dead account?"

"I'm Petrakova Selle. I swear, I was told it was fine," Isobel gasped.

Pizzette hit the man's arm. "Let her go."

He was already reaching to call the police. "I don't know who you are, but..." He stopped short, bringing Isobel's face right in front of his. "God, it's—"

Mattie grabbed Isobel's legs and pulled. She tumbled out of the man's grasp and onto the floor. I kicked open the doors, and we took to the streets. He stumbled after us but was quickly lost in the dark.

We ran past the trash-processing yard and the slum neighborhoods. Past the fountain in the center of the city. We only stopped short of the palace because Isobel had hurt her ankle.

"Five minutes," Mattie panted, dropping to her knees. "We can breathe."

"Let me see your foot," Pizzette said, pulling Isobel's foot into her lap. "Oh, it's swollen."

"It'll be fine. It's an old injury. Marmi said my foot has always been this way." Isobel covered her face with her hands. "I didn't know that account was so big. There was so much money on it."

"Why did Marmi have the information for the Nolatores' account?" I asked. "I've never heard of them, but they must have been pretty famous."

Isobel shrugged. "I'm sorry. You were already going to pay, but I wanted to be nice."

"It's okay. That driver was pissing us off," Pizzette said, placing Isobel's foot back on the ground and standing up. "Mattie, what's the plan when we get to the palace?"

"I'll head to my lab. Everything we need is there." Mattie pressed her fists against her cheeks, groaning. "I hope Inger didn't somehow call a helicopter down to Pigladen and beat us to it."

"Do you think anyone knows we're coming?" Pizzette questioned, rubbing her elbows. "Oh, it's so cold."

The bus and its heater had been a distraction. We all fled without cloaks, and Cyan's wintry rain was unforgiving.

"That gives us more incentive to hurry," I said. "Isobel, I can carry you on my back."

I wondered how obvious it was that I was lying. Isobel was more than half my height, and probably weight as well.

"I'm fine." Isobel murmured. "We can keep running."

Running. I did not know why I could not shake the feeling that this was going too smoothly. I had never known a Cyan to waste time when they had an objective, and Inger's absence was unsettling.

Just stay focused. No need to start being paranoid when you're already in enough danger.

***

Pizzette

Cyan's palace was a looming shadow against the black curtain of night, more terrifying than it was on the first day of Etiquette. We all froze in the street leading to the gates, doubt finally getting the best of us.

"I think I see Inger," Luck murmured, crossing her arms and shivering. The rain was only making us more miserable, melting what was left of the snow and chilling us to the core.

"Wave." I took a deep breath and continued up the walkway. "Mattie, you should be in front. The guards know you're an advisor. They'll let you in."

"Hopefully they went in for the night, so we can avoid mishaps." Mattie hurried in front of me, her muddied clothing and messy hair convincing no one of her status. "Sometimes they get bored and leave. I mean, the only person they're guarding here is Inger."

"Not anyone important," Luck added under her breath, pulling Isobel to her side. "Stop walking so far away from us. You might make a run for it."

"I'm not sure I'm ready to go back."

"Well this is a bad place to still be deciding," Luck mumbled, ruffling Isobel's soggy hair. "This is your home. You've lived here before, but you don't remember."

"Don't remind her," I snapped. "This is hard enough already."

"I was being realistic, Pizzette."

"Guys." Mattie glared at us, the first time she had lost her temper. "Be quiet and let me do the talking. We won't make it in as a bickering crowd of dirty, lost girls."

"Maybe I should have brought my nonexistent ID card," Luck whispered. Isobel and I laughed behind our hands, so Mattie did not yell at us again.

The grand gates came into view, towering over our heads. The top of the pointed frame was already rusting, despite its frequent alterations. No one cared about this palace anymore, not without their ruling family in it.

Adding to our good fortune were the recognizable faces of the two guards. I forgot I was supposed to be quiet and bounded up to them. "Clint. Tomas. This is a rather perfect occasion."

Clint held up a hand. "Lady, wait."

I nearly tripped when Mattie grabbed my arm, pulling me back. On the other side of the gate was a slumped-over body.

My elation quickly turned to fear.

"Guys, what did you do?" I whispered.

"Don't be afraid of us," Tomas said in a quavering voice. "Of me anyway. It's Bonne. Clint attacked him."

"Tomas, you skipped over some important details." Clint tried to appeal to Mattie and Luck, who had both turned vicious in seconds.

Luck's fiery eyes alone could have set the palace ablaze once more. "He was going to attack you. Inger told us you were coming. She wanted the guards to detain you."

Luck placed herself in front of Isobel, her defensive stance never dropping. "Is this a setup? Are people going to grab us from behind?"

Tomas tried to step in. "Mattie, you know me. I would never stand next to Clint if I thought he was lying."

Mattie considered it, and her hold on my arm loosened. "Why are you risking your lives then? You shouldn't be—"

"Is that her?" Tomas asked, peeking around Luck's shoulder. "The princess?"

"Yeah," I said.

"Pizzette, don't share everything," Luck groaned.

"It's too late now." I looked at the guards again, my doubts dwindling. "Can you help us?"

"They better," Luck growled.

"Why did you come here in the middle of the night? You're all covered in mud." Clint stepped forward, inspecting my face carefully. "There's a fresh wound on your face. You can never stay out of trouble."

Clint was forever going to fret over me, and…it did not annoy me. I was grateful he had even noticed. Cared about my well-being.

"That's not important. We need to go to Mattie's lab and collect evidence to prove that Inger caused the Burning and was hiding the fact that Isobel survived."

Clint and Tomas exchanged a look. Maybe they had some form of telepathy that only guards could understand because they started putting together a plan on the spot.

"I'll take Mattie up to the lab. You have to hide the others," Tomas started.

"We can wait inside the school building. Make it fast."

"It's best if we don't split up," Luck said, still unsure of them. "Right, girls?"

"Fine, but we have to hurry." Clint pushed me ahead of him. "Should one of us stay so Inger doesn't suspect anything?"

"You stay but move Bonne somewhere." Tomas tried to sound sure of himself.

"Don't get them captured. Stick to back halls and don't make a sound." Clint looked at me. "You in particular."

***

Mattie

We filed into the palace behind Tomas. It felt like all eyes in the country were watching us through the closed windows, ready to call Inger the second we stepped into the lab. As expected, some of the guards had left their posts. At least this part would be easy.

"So," Tomas whispered as he unlocked the front doors. "How did you find yourselves with the princess of Cyan?"

"A well-timed convenience." *And some hairs left in a child-sized hat.*

"I never would have guessed that she was right here the entire time. I guess we've always thought the solution to our problems was miles away." Tomas looked over his shoulder at her and smiled. "Hello."

Isobel waved. Luck was the only person who was still closed off to Tomas and Clint. I did not understand why she made it a point to act intimidating. She was no giant, but her glare was scary enough.

We walked through darkness and silence, the footsteps of guards in adjacent hallways the only thing keeping us grounded. Exhaustion was finally catching up with me, but I refused to let it slow me down. These would be the last few hours of Inger's reign.

My lab was as clean as I had left it. Everyone stood to the side while I gathered the evidence I left behind. Notes and summaries of tests I ran on Isobel's DNA. The video recorder from the meeting I was supposed to edit so it looked false. I checked everything over, hoping what I had was enough. It seemed like the discovery was made by someone else over a century ago. Everything I touched could have been made of shadows.

"Ready?" Luck asked, shaking out her wet hair. "This place is making me claustrophobic. Do you really spend all of your time here?"

"It's not a small lab." Her critique did not apply to my spacious lab, but now was not the time to argue about the size.

"Should we call a cab to the Radio Tower?" Pizzette asked, her eyes widening at the sight of all my equipment. Was she amazed that I knew how to use it all and did so much research? I'd never impressed anyone but Inger before.

"That's too risky. A car on the road at this hour would turn heads everywhere." Tomas put his hand on my shoulder, guiding me to the door. "I'll walk you."

"It's on the other side of the city." His offer seemed marvelous, and the comforting warmth of his hands almost convinced me, but I did not want to put him in any more danger. "If Inger returns, she'll know you helped us. If this all fails, I don't want you hurt."

"I...Don't worry about me." Tomas eyed Isobel. "Worry about our princess."

He draped his coat over my shoulders as we entered the hallway, surrounding me in a perpetual hug.

"What is that video anyway?" Luck pushed ahead and took the box out of my hands. "What's it proving?"

I tried to take it back from her. "Luck, you do not want to see that. It deserves to be destroyed once this is over."

Luck switched it on anyway. I yanked Isobel away before she could see anything. It was not long before Luck's face paled and she shut the recorder.

"She's the devil," Luck whispered. "The absolute worst."

Tomas's eyes met mine. His were filled with worry, concerned about what I let myself endure by siding with Inger this whole time. He might have gotten a glimpse of the video, but it did not matter. In a few hours, the whole world was going to see these tapes. The truth.

We rounded a dark corner, the only light coming from two enormous windows someone had left cracked open. Dust fluttered from the panes as I lifted it, scanning the courtyard to make sure Clint was still in position.

He was, and Bonne's body no longer blocked the entry, but an enormous black car had just pulled up to the front, its doors open and spilling guests onto the walkway while I watched.

Pizzette gasped behind me, but the sound barely registered.

Inger stepped out of the car, tossing her hair over shoulder. Next to her, Norm was polishing his knife and looking bored.

They were here.

Inger was here.

***

Part 6

Pizzette

"Change of plans. We have to split up," Mattie said quickly, backing away from the window before one of them had the bright idea to look up.

Tomas and Luck protested earnestly.

"It's unsafe," Luck hissed. "They have weapons."

"One of us needs to carry the evidence while the rest create a diversion," Mattie continued, reorganizing her notes and clipping them together.

"We should all split the evidence," I suggested. "And Isobel should stick with Tomas."

"You should *all* stay with me," Tomas said frantically. "Mattie, think this through."

"I did," Mattie said. "Pizzette, take the evidence and get out of here with Isobel. The rest of us are going to slow Inger down."

"No," Luck roared. "She's going to lose it."

Isobel's hand latched onto mine, dissolving my arguments immediately.

"Pizzette is the sneakiest one out of us. She'll find a way."

"I don't even know where the Radio Tower is," I mumbled.

"I'll show you," Isobel said confidently, tugging my hand. "We have to go."

"Wait." Tomas checked the window again, swearing. "They're already coming inside. Mattie, all of us need to leave."

"We can't overpower her," Mattie said in a level voice. "So, we let her think she's won. If we all appear to have some form of evidence, she won't know who to target first. Smuggling out Isobel is the most important task."

"God," Luck breathed. "This better work."

"You're agreeing to this?" Tomas cried.

"I have nothing better." Luck's green eyes landed on me. "Don't mess this up, or I'll never come around to liking you or our miserable families."

I frowned back at her. "Don't screw up your part either."

Mattie kept the cover of the recorder tucked under one arm. "This is so I can pretend it's the real thing."

"What should I do?" Tomas interrupted her again, bent on making sure she would not leave. His concern for her was so obvious, and it was not even directed at me. Somehow, Mattie looked past it, focused on achieving her one task, almost like she had no idea how to address his emotions. *Her* emotions.

"Go back downstairs and act like you have not seen anything tonight," Mattie whispered, lightly touching his face. "Please?" For a second, she looked like she was near tears, like the events of the last ten years suddenly hit her at once.

Royal Advisor, Lady Matilda. The conviction in her voice would have made any stranger listen. Somehow, even covered in mud and standing at the edge of danger, she kept herself together, well enough to demand that everyone listen. If I did not know any better, I would have mistaken her for Isobel's equal.

"Alright." Tomas's hands closed around hers. "Be careful, Mattie."

And everyone else...oh. I glanced over at Luck, who for half a second looked annoyed, then realized what was going on.

I wondered if Mattie did too.

She simply nodded, then she and Luck took off down the hallway, leaving me alone with Tomas and the princess of Cyan.

***

"Search the courtyard. I bet they're already running toward the tower," Inger snapped, opening her carpetbag, seeking more Preserv pills. She had not felt this strong in forever, completely in control of her gift, her curse. She gulped down a handful, the surge of buried power hot and energizing. "We will not camp out at the tower and create a scene." She held her breath, letting the Preserv clear the fog in her mind, letting her dampened gift reform.

She sensed the tension in Clint's set shoulders, heard the grumblings in his thoughts that betrayed the lies he told them. Even now, with her back to him, she could feel his unease.

"Oh, they're still inside the palace." *There it is shock all over his face.* Inger chuckled, smiling at him over her shoulder. "Thank you, Clint."

"Madame, I never spoke?" His voice was fighting to stay level.

"You didn't need to." Inger motioned to Norm and Arabella. "Arabella, you take the left side. Norm, come with me."

Arabella smirked, wiping her blade on her leg. "This'll be fun, just like in the old days."

Inger nodded. "Jessica and the Daniels will take the easy route to the tower. We'll be behind you soon."

Clint whirled around, drawing his gun in a flash.

Inger had him pinned in place in half the time, the horrible delusion clouding his eyes unseen by others but very real to him. She dug into the deepest recesses of his mind, seeking the fears he held closest. *They tormented me for years. Don't expect that girl to come to your aid now.* She left him rambling, yelling at the nothingness in front of them while Norm followed her out through the gate.

"Haven't seen the nightmares in forever," Norm said under his breath as he helped her through. "What's he seeing?"

"His regrets coming back to haunt him." Inger's eyes danced. "Don't we all have those?"

"Not after today. You'll be queen."

"Right." Inger took one last look at the palace. Here she was, dressed in awful muddy clothes, looking like the Inger that was cast away by the Lagardes years ago, the one that had almost thought her purpose in life was gone. *To win. That's all they ever wanted me for.*

This palace has always belonged to me. Today, they will finally know.

"Be ready to strike," Inger yelled. "Four insolent children will not stop me now."

***

Luck

Just a month ago, I was shopping for expensive gowns with Mama, so I could attend one of the best schools in the country, without a thought for my future. Everything seemed fine, until I stepped into that school. Locked eyes with Inger.

Now, I was pressed against the smooth granite wall of the palace, the overgrown weeds tickling my bare muddy legs, icy rain soaking my shoulders. Inger's voice was unmistakable, as was Clint's desperate yelling. *What is happening?*

Arabella was stalking the courtyard, the others not far ahead. I had to move farther away from the side exit before she found me. I had to make sure at least one of us got to the tower before Inger, so our story had a chance of getting out.

"Where are you?" Arabella screamed, suddenly very close.

It was now or never. In the dark I would be harder to see. I leaned back into the wall, and then charged forward.

Arabella immediately fell into line behind me. I turned quickly, seeking the gate. The only part that allowed access to the outside was blocked, so I barreled straight into it, trying to hoist myself up and over.

I was too late. Arabella grabbed me around the waist and threw me to the ground. I scrambled back on all fours, slipping in a puddle. She was above me in a second, her knife raised and ready.

"You won't win," I said as loudly as I dared. "You know it all ends here."

"Have you seen Cyan?" Arabella laughed, grabbing my hair, and lifting me up. "They'll believe whatever shoddy explanation we feed them tomorrow."

"You must not know Cyan the way I do."

"Exactly, you stupid, ignorant child, the way you see this country is all wrong. It's the fanciful way you were brought up, a life of excess and everything you could ever want handed to you. You never saw this city crumble, and you will never experience what we did."

I was at a loss for words, digging into the ground and trying to pull myself away. "I don't believe you."

"That's not my—"

I saw a burst of red, and then the recorder's box hit the side of Arabella's head. She fell to the side, swearing.

"Run," Mattie yelled as she zipped past.

Arabella was hunched over, clutching her head and groaning.

I wasted no time getting back to my feet, and ran like hell, my heels nearly smoking.

***

Pizzette

"Isobel, come here," I hissed into the dark. The evidence was in a sad pile in my arms, somehow not flying to the ground despite my trembling. I pointed to the window I had opened and tossed out the rope of sheets Tomas knotted together before running back downstairs. "We're climbing out."

Isobel nodded, adjusting her bracelet so it was not lost on her upper arm. "Help me down?"

"Yeah." I swung my legs over the sill, wondering if I was ready to do this. I set the pile down for a second and reached for the rope, praying it would hold my weight. It swayed below me, but the knots stayed tight.

Oh God, please help me. I steadied myself, pushing the evidence a little farther from the edge.

"Okay Isobel, you can stand on my head and hold the evidence in one hand."

Her feet settled on my head timidly. I heard the pile scrape against the sill, then she was holding it, pressed into her chest and shivering. *This kid is insanely brave.*

"Don't look down. It's only four stories," I said, more to myself as I began to climb down, my feet padding against the side of the palace and the windows. In the dark we were shadows, barely visible in the wind-blown rain. The rope swung above and below us, threatening to send us falling prematurely with every gust of wind. I held my breath the entire time, only focusing on keeping Isobel steady. She switched the evidence to one hand and held the rope with the other, squeezing her eyes shut and whispering something in French under her breath over and over.

One of my hands slipped. I jerked backward, flailing to catch hold again. Isobel's presence disappeared above me for two seconds.

"Isobel," I screamed. "Isobel!"

The rain cleared. She was still dangling above me, clutching the rope with one hand like it was gold while her feet kicked the air.

"I'm right here." I reached up with one hand and caught her foot, steadying her. "I'm sorry. My hand slipped. I almost dropped us."

Isobel's response was lost by another puff of wind. Both of us screamed, the rope starting to give.

Without thinking, I wrapped my ankle around a bunch of sheets and grabbed Isobel. We were only supported by her hand and my foot now, but at least she was not fighting to stay connected anymore.

"We're going to be okay," I yelled. "There isn't much left."

I slid down as safely as I could, the knots above us giving up after thirty seconds.

We were *falling*.

The ground tackled us, knocking the breath out of me. Isobel flew out of my arms, landing somewhere in the grass a few feet away.

I struggled to my feet, vision blurring. The rest of the rope landed in a coiled pile next to me.

Isobel pushed herself up onto her feet, giving me a halfhearted thumbs-up sign. "I'm okay."

"We have to keep moving." I directed her over to the fence, lifting her over my head so she could climb over first. I followed, barely paying attention to whether anyone saw us. The rain was ghastly now, falling in thick sheets and making me frigid.

"I know where it is," Isobel said, pointing at an empty street. "This is the fastest way."

I followed her, ignoring the burning in my legs. If she was brave enough to trust me to carry her down a rope of knotted sheets, I had to ignore discomfort for her sake.

The city was ghostly at night, all the bars and shops I had thought would be open giving the appearance of being closed, all the windows dark on the lower floors. It was only the penthouse and rooftops that had any lights, and even then, the noise was minimal. It was as if there was some pre-established curfew everyone kept to very strictly.

Either way, there was no one to help us right now.

We ran past the sheriff's station. I swore when one of their cars began to follow us.

***

Mattie

Lady Arabella fell over, swearing and holding a hand to her temple. I had never known her to have headaches, but she looked absolutely distraught for a moment.

Luck bounded away. I relaxed, the empty box falling to the ground with a *thump*.

Then a bandana was wrapped over my eyes, the motion so violent I fell backwards into Norm. "Gotcha, little lab rat."

My knees wobbled as he knotted my wrists together. *This is it for me. At least I gave Pizzette the evidence. I hope they make it.*

"Thought you could outsmart us?" He slapped my cheek hard. I swallowed my sob, squaring my shoulders and raising my chin. "Don't look so defiant. Inger has plans for you."

"You ought to kill me now before I tattle," I whispered, receiving a sharp kick to the back of the knee.

"Inger's going to speak to you first. No one gets off easy." He pulled me by the arm, my foot bumping into someone else's as we passed them. When the blindfold was lifted a few minutes later, Inger was right in front of me.

"I won't tell you anything," I said quietly.

"I already know your plan," Inger spat. "The Radio Tower? What a terribly obvious place to go."

"My friends will make it," I fired back. "The real ruler will be crowned."

"*Lady* Matilda, are you sure you do not want that title for yourself? Friends? Who would call you, such a socially challenged idiot, their friend?"

Her comments stung. "Of course not. I know I'm no queen, not even noble. I'm not doing this for malicious reasons."

"No, you want to be someone's hero. You want everyone to love you, right?" Inger lifted her eyebrows as if I should consider what she was telling me to be true. "This gives you a place."

"I'm fine where I am," I muttered. "I know that outside my lab I have no life."

"You're still lying to yourself. Poor and scrawny. You long to be wanted by anyone who takes you, even if it means disobeying your leader, the woman who saved you from a life of begging on the streets."

"Well no one wants you either," I griped, kicking at her. "That's why Prince Indio chose Cyrana instead of you."

Inger screamed, lunging for me. "You don't understand anything. None of us had a choice."

Norm heaved me up, tossing me into the side of the car. My shoulder took the worst of it, as I failed to catch myself falling. I whimpered for a second, taking a moment to realize he'd pulled me out of the way of Inger's attack.

"You should send her to Mortem," Arabella said, walking up behind Inger. "Give her a life sentence."

"No," Inger said with a frown. "Let her test the limits of her own stupidity. She thinks she's invincible." She grabbed my chin, opening my mouth and forcing a handful of mystery pills down my throat. They burned going down. I barely had the energy left to scream for help before the darkness pulled me under.

***

Luck

I sat back on my heels, chest heaving.

They had Mattie. She looked unnaturally still as they lifted her into the back of their car and drove off, leaving the palace behind in disarray.

I had to stall them. Pizzette and Isobel were on foot and would never beat a car.

I ran to Clint who was curled up on his side, a grown man muttering under his breath and looking at something over my shoulder.

"Fire. I can't save anyone. I can't..."

"Snap out of it," I yelled, slapping his face. "They have Mattie. I need help."

What had Inger done to him? I did not see any physical marks on his body, but his mental state was damaged.

My yelling was futile. There was no way to shake him out of it.

My eyes landed on his belt, at the various weapons clipped on it. *Dear Lord.*

"Clint, I'm going to borrow one of these," I whispered, reaching across his body and unhooking one of his guns. It felt awful and dangerous in my hands. "Tell me how this works."

"I missed him...the diamond..."

"Come on." I blinked tears out of my eyes, shaking him hard. "Tell me how this works. They're getting away."

"Luck!" My head snapped up. Through the rain I could see Tomas running across the courtyard. Guards filled the doorway he left open behind him, confused.

I started crying. "They took Mattie."

Tomas knelt next to me, carefully taking the gun out of my hands. "Which way?"

"Into the city. I didn't see anything." I wiped my eyes with already wet hands, the cold relentless. "What are we going to do?"

"We have to stop the car." Tomas helped me to my feet, looking at Clint in confusion. "What's wrong with him?"

"I found him like this. I don't know what happened."

Tomas turned to the other guards, giving out orders like a captain. "Take him inside. Something's wrong." They obeyed like sheep, flooding the courtyard in seconds.

He picked me up, setting me on his shoulders. His shyness was deceptive, hiding the fact that despite his gentle demeanor, he was built like a guard through and through. "We'll be faster this way."

We slipped through the gate before the wind blew it shut, catching the car just before it disappeared.

Tomas sprinted down the drive. *Mattie. He's as scared as I am that they're going to hurt her.*

He reached up, pressing the gun into my hands delicately. "Pull the trigger when I tell you too. We have to blow the tires."

"I think they see us." Someone's face was watching through the back window, but I could not be sure what they saw past the storm. "Tomas, someone is looking."

"Now," he said, pulling my hand downward so my aim was more accurate. "Press it."

I did, and the blast that shot from it nearly knocked us over. I swayed, Tomas grabbing my back to steady me before I hit the ground.

One of the tires started going flat, the car spinning out of control.

"Again, Luck. Hit them again."

I sniffled, wiping my eyes again. "I...I..."

The back window rolled down. Without a warning, they started shooting back at us.

***

Pizzette

"Don't slip," Isobel yelled in front of me. "Just stay to the side of the road."

Oh Cyan, there's nothing like being chased by the police in the rain during the early hours of morning.

Despite Isobel's motivation, the officer caught up with us.

"Stop," I whispered, reaching for her shoulder. "There's no point. Maybe they can give us a ride."

Isobel nodded, but she was not convinced.

The officer slowed behind us, yelling from inside their heated car. "What are you two doing in the streets during a storm early in the morning?"

"Some people are trying to hurt us," Isobel explained. "We're trying to get away from them."

"Who? I'll have to send police their way. Sit inside and warm up for a moment." The side doors opened, welcoming us with soft seats and warmth.

"We can't be too specific," I said, itching to dive inside. "But…can you take us to the Radio Tower?"

"Can I?" The officer stepped out of the car, their voice familiar without the screen in the way. *"Can I?"*

I took a step back, my gasp buried in my throat.

The officer was Mr. Daniels.

Isobel kicked his leg and then took off. I followed, cursing myself for even stopping.

A bullet flew past my ear. I screamed, nearly colliding with a street sign.

"He has a gun, Isobel. Run in front of me." His car was gaining on us, the siren on and lights flashing.

She listened, taking the evidence from my hands as well. She was only partially protected, and her feet were starting to slow down. It was only the slippery streets and the wind obscuring our vision that kept any space between us and Mr. Daniels, although that distance was closing in.

"How are we going to stop him?" Isobel yelled.

I veered off the street toward the gated neighborhoods, an idea coming to mind that might end horribly. "We have to trap him somewhere. He's going to run us over."

As if he could hear us, the car sped up. Isobel and I dove onto opposite sides of the street.

She started running behind the car, trying to sneak around the side. Out of nowhere, it reversed, barely missing her. Mr. Daniels backed up again.

I tackled Isobel out of the way. Both of us hit the street, rainwater splashing up from the puddles. The car was still coming.

"I'm going to my house," I whispered, scrambling to my feet. "Follow me."

Tumbleweed Gardens was the only part of the city I bothered to remember since going there was a vacation away from school. Mr. Daniels followed our zig-zagging pattern like a shadow, never missing a turn though we tried to confuse him. The car was faster, but he was trying to follow two small targets in the dark, the only reason we were still alive.

We approached the neighborhood on the northern outskirts of the city. Mr. Daniels was behind us, gaining speed exponentially.

"Climb over the fence and jump into the bushes," I yelled, lifting Isobel up and over my head. "He won't see it in the dark."

We dove into the bushes just as the car hit the fence. Metal screeched. The tires slipped as he belatedly tried to reverse, and then the whole thing was sliding down toward my house.

Everything stopped at the base of the hill, making a terrible noise as it collided with one of the overgrown trees. The lights came on, and I knew Mom had to be panicking inside.

Mr. Daniels did not mind that. I saw him push open the side door and crawl out, looking crazed as he started sauntering up the hill.

"Move," I snapped, picking up the recorder and the files and rising to my feet.

Isobel was quiet.

"Isobel, what is it?" I knelt next to her. "We have to keep moving, he's coming back up already."

"My…ankle hurts," she wheezed. "When I jumped…I fell too quickly."

Damn. I shook my head, the pain clustering all around now. "I'll carry you." She was a skinny child, but I was not necessarily strong myself.

Isobel held the evidence, and I managed to hold her so her leg was not dangling.

"Almost there?" Isobel whispered.

"Yeah. We just need a cab."

***

"We are on route to the tower. This road looks clear. Less puddles." Norm spun the wheel wildly, his face completely focused. "Do you think Miscellaneous caught up with them?"

"Not in this storm," Arabella muttered, massaging her forehead. "We can barely see five feet in front of us."

"He's not a perceptive driver," Inger said sharply. "Norm trained several years of his life for an occasion like this one."

"I enjoyed none of that," Norm said, making another hazardous turn.

"By the way, are we still being followed?" Inger asked off-handedly.

"I don't see anyone, but then again, all I can see is rain." Arabella mumbled some other sarcastic comments Inger chose to ignore. "Should I keep shooting?"

"Wait until we make some more distance. They should tire out easily."

"Palace guards aren't supposed to tire out easily anymore," Arabella said with a laugh. "You remember the happy days when they barely noticed a thing?"

"It's always been the same. Pathetic." Inger turned her eyes back to the road, doubt settling in her chest. The Daniels should have updated her by now. Jessica and Miscellanea were supposed to already be at the tower, having stolen a cab to get there. Miscellaneous was supposed to have captured Isobel and had the evidence in her custody by now. No one was calling Inger yet, and she was starting to panic. "I'm wondering if Cyan's curriculum enforces too much physical education. How did an eight-year-old outrun a moving car?"

"Isobel is not a normal eight-year-old," Norm said, his face never changing as he accelerated and blew through several stop lights. "If anything, she's *stronger*."

Inger growled, swatting his arm. "She's a failure. Have you seen anything remarkable in her yet? I believe the doctor made a mistake when he allowed Cyrana to have a child."

"Actually, his first mistake was Cyrana," Arabella started to say.

"*Actually*, his first mistake was me, and then my sister." Inger scratched her arm, sweating. "God, I would roll down this window if the damn rain would stop for once."

"Rain in December," Arabella mused. "That's about as sad and depressing as our regular lives."

"Remember the first time we saw the sun?" Norm muttered with a smirk.

"No, because it never shows up in Cyan," Inger answered, hitting his arm again. "Arabella, is Mattie still unconscious?"

"Yeah. You really knocked her out with that concoction." Arabella poked Mattie's forehead, frowning. "Why is she still alive? Are you really thinking about Plan B?"

Norm took his eyes off the road and looked at Inger, concerned.

"Yes," she said, biting her lip. "If we cannot stop them, we have to take over Cyan the other way. The much more complicated and political way."

***

Pizzette

I had no clue how to drive, but we had a cab that accepted the payment information I entered. I wondered how much it would withdraw from Mom's account if I ran it into a wall.

"Do you think someone will be mad that we stole their car?" Isobel asked from the backseat, her injured foot elevated on the cushion further down the seat.

"They left it unlocked, so that's not our problem." I checked the rearview mirror for Mr. Daniels, and then switched the cab on, the engine making our location known. If he was lost before, he had a clear destination now. "They'll be happy they helped save the princess."

Isobel laughed dryly. "Princess. That's a new name."

"I'm sorry. This is all really new, and it's overwhelming, but this is your... destiny." *Who am I kidding? I don't have any reasonable advice to give someone in her position.*

"I just want to be Petrakova again. That was simpler. Not Isobel. Not Princess Lagarde." Isobel covered her face with her hands, the pearl bracelet glimmering in the moonlight.

The car suddenly accelerated under us, barreling down the street and making both of us scream. My hands found the wheel and we swerved onto a muddy street leading to the south end of the city. We coasted for a while, my clumsy starting and stopping throwing us all around each time I almost drove off the road. The rain was a blanket now, covering everything with an unforgiving mist and making me tear up in fright.

Somehow, we made it to the sloping streets of the south side without any incidents, muddy water cascading down all the slushy paths.

"Up the hills," Isobel called out. "Keep driving up, then you'll see the sign."

I slammed my foot on the pedal, cringing as mud swirled around the tires and splashed on the windows. The car cried, but slowly it climbed up the hills.

Pop! Bang!

"Isobel, head down," I shouted as the window next to me shattered. My heart pounded as rain poured into the car, plastering my sleeves to my arms. I checked the rearview mirror before it exploded too, seeing Mr. Daniels and Miss Daniels driving another cab behind us. A gun poked out of one of their windows, punching holes into the sides of the cab. "If I'm hit, take the evidence and run," I told Isobel. "I mean it. Run like you have nothing else left."

"I'm not leaving you." Isobel peered out the back window before it broke, squealing and falling back down. "How can we stop them?"

"We can't. We're just going to keep driving." I sounded triumphant, but I was terrified. I wanted this to stop. I wanted to go home to Bark and sleep for days. Forget this horrible country and its horrible leader.

"Run him over," Isobel screamed. "Let the car roll, then we step out and run the rest of the way there."

"I'd have to carry you," I argued weakly.

"Fine. He's going to hit us." Isobel met my eyes and nodded, determined.

"Put your belt on," I said, moving the gear the wrong way first, fixing it, and then letting go of the brakes. Gravity took over.

Everything was in slow motion. My head flung back into the leather headrest. Another window cracked, spiderwebs spreading in three blinks of the eye. I felt pain shoot through my arm like a slow river, radiating from my shoulder. The recorder hit the side of the car, and Isobel sailed out of her seat to catch it, hitting the ground heavily. The water kept flooding the car as if it was trying to drown us all…

Boom. We bowled into something large and heavy and kept sliding. Isobel tumbled out of her door, followed by me.

I grabbed her hand before she fell further, and both of us watched the cars crash at the bottom. Just a smoky, crumpled heap of metal at this point. There was no way of knowing if anyone was inside. *I hope to God they found a way to sneak out again. I'm no killer.*

Isobel's voice was shrill. "Inger's coming. That's her car."

My head spun, a headache roaring behind my eyes. My left arm was limp at my side, bogged down by the piece of flyaway glass that had been embedded in it. "Okay, give me a second…"

"I can see her." Isobel was crying, blood pouring down her face from a cut on her forehead. "We're so close, come on." She wrapped her arms around my middle, trying to lift me up. "Pizzette?"

Is this what it feels like when you've reached the end? At this point, do you know you're going to die?

I pushed myself up on shaking arms, coughing water out of my lungs. *Choking. Choking on flames and smoke and whatever else kills you here.*

"Please, stand up," Isobel wailed, shaking my shoulder. "Please."

***

Luck

We followed the car all the way to the hill. I thought we would continue until Tomas collapsed, gasping for air.

I fell next to him, the gun flying out of my hands into the dark. "Tomas—"

"I'm fine," he said quickly. "Out of breath, but fine. You have to keep going."

I shook my head. "I can't stop them on my own."

He handed me one of his heavier knives, pointing in the direction of their parked cars. Inger, Norm, and Arabella were dashing up the hill toward Isobel and Pizzette. Mattie was nowhere to be seen.

I wrapped my hands around his, pulling him to his feet. It was selfish, but even with him barely able to breathe, I needed him next to me. I was too scared to go into the fight alone.

"Tomas, we're almost there."

"Don't let me slow you down." He coughed into his shoulder, his entire body quaking. "Have you seen Mattie?"

"No." I blinked my eyes quickly, tears mixing with the rain on my face. "Are we really going to attack them from behind?"

"I will. You need to catch up with the others." Tomas nudged me forward. "Go on. I'll keep them off your tail."

"Wait. Are you really going to fight *Norm*?"

He nodded, taking a labored breath. "Time is running out, Luck. You have to move."

I would never be able to thank him properly. "Tomas…I don't know what to say but…"

"It's okay. Go ahead of me."

The hill was an uphill trudge. I nearly fell, the muddy rainwater almost carrying me away with it. *Whoever said I was small should see me now.*

Inger was ahead of me, yelling out orders for the others to shoot Isobel. I could barely see her on the ground next to a crumpled form, desperately trying to rouse whoever that was.

Without another thought, I ran toward them.

Arabella gasped in surprise when I grabbed her from behind. Norm and Inger whirled around, each snatching a leg and pulling me away. Norm nearly broke my arm swinging me onto the ground, stealing the knife from my hand.

"Do we need this one?" he asked Inger breathlessly.

"No."

Tomas slammed into Norm before he could act, snatching the knife back and tossing it to me before facing Norm again. I wriggled away, and then ran to Isobel before Arabella could reach her.

"Get out of my way, idiot," Arabella snapped, smacking me across the face.

Isobel was on her feet now, making a run for the Radio Tower. I jumped in between her and Arabella, holding her back while Isobel limped as she ran toward the tower. Tomas and Norm were still fighting with each other. Mattie and Inger had gone missing.

I spotted Inger walking up the hill in the direction of the princess, armed and reeling with anger.

Without any regard for my safety, I charged up the hill after her.

***

The girl of many names struggled up the hill, the determination clear on her face.

Petrakova Selle tripped, stumbling to her knee.

Marmi's daughter picked herself up, twisted ankle aching.

Isobel held the evidence like it was a lifeline and continued her limping up towards her goal.

Princess Lagarde knew that sacrifices had been made for her, and that the only way to merit honor was to continue fighting the evil that had almost destroyed her home.

Inger then grabbed her arm, holding a knife close to her neck.

"I was weak then. I should have finished you off myself. Hesitation will always be my downfall," Inger sneered, her arm tensing as she betrayed her own conviction.

The one of luck, but mostly misfortune, hit her over the head with the blunt edge of her knife.

Isobel Lagarde took Lady Lucienne's hand, and they ran the rest of the way to the tower.

Part 7

Mattie

The fire burned beneath my eyelids, filling my vision with smoky gray. My fingers twitched, tendrils of a light blaze wafting off them. They felt impossibly hot.

My heart was racing, my mouth dry. Everywhere was smoking, covered in flames.

It was Lady Arabella who pried open my eyes, forcing me to stand. Then she punched me in the face. My head flew back, the gray sky greeting me. I heard sirens in the distance, wailing in time with my rampant pulse.

Sobs. Someone was crying, screaming at Inger to leave them alone.

I held a hand to my nose, startled when it came away spotting red.

"She wakes up so slowly," Lady Arabella complained to Inger, who had her arm around Norm's shoulders. "Her eyes are still focusing."

"We need to keep moving," Inger growled. "Into the tree line before the police find us."

Norm pulled me off the hood of the car in one abrupt motion, my knees banging against the ground while I fumbled to stand. *What's going on? Where is everyone?*

"Inger, whatever you gave her was too strong," Norm said reproachfully. "I'm not carrying her."

"She'll snap out of it." Inger looked like three shadows when she walked in front of me, grabbing Miss Daniels by the ear. "Stand up now. They'll be coming out of the tower soon. They ran like chickens when they were on their own, but with the police backing them, we have no support."

"Plan B," Lady Arabella murmured, pressing three fingers against her forehead.

"The story already broke?" Norm asked, pointing up at the sky. "It's only been half an hour."

Half an hour? Since when? How long was I out? I carefully stood up, bracing myself against the side of the crushed car. The downpour had ended, but not before it put out the flames.

Flames. Everything begins and ends in flames.

I jerked my hand away from the wreckage without thinking, a whimper escaping me. Both Inger and Norm turned and looked at me analytically.

"Did you remember something?" Inger barked, cheeks going red.

I shook my head. *Like what?*

Miss Daniels threw her hands up and cried again, batting Inger's hands away. "He's dead," she sobbed, wiping her face with her cold and stiff hands.

Lady Arabella walked around to the other side of the car. Miss Jessica was crumpled on the ground, her ever-serious face squashed in a puddle of mud.

"She's unconscious," Lady Arabella said with a careless shrug. "Less deadweight. Oh, sorry Miscellanea."

Miss Daniels planted herself next to Mr. Daniels' prone body. "I'm not leaving him. You can't make me."

"He's dead," Lady Arabella snapped. "He already left us all."

Miss Daniels shook her head. Without exchanging a word, Norm, Inger, and Lady Arabella simply looked at each other, nodded, and then started to walk away.

"Mattie don't play any games," Inger growled.

Out of habit, I started to follow them.

We disappeared into the trees surrounding the city, the thick leaves quickly concealing the rest of the hills and the tower. In a few minutes, the noise of a city waking up to chaos and conspiracy was gone, replaced by our heavy feet.

"We failed," Norm said quietly, walking well despite his wounded leg. "We're really going to walk away from them? I could so easily break down their barricade and kill them all."

Inger giggled maniacally. "I can't have such *carnage* to clean up, although it would be faster. I have another plan, one that hinges on the silly agreement King Idrick and Queen Isobel reached shortly before the rebels stormed the palace."

Rebels storming the palace? I coughed, and suddenly the three of them were interested in me again.

"Do you have something you need to say?" Norm grumbled. "I didn't hear it the first time."

"Idrick and Isobel honestly were the downfall of this country," Inger said, dragging her hand along a passing tree branch. It snapped back, nearly hitting Lady Arabella in the face. "Imagine how desperate they were to write up such a charter, knowing that one day their home would be attacked." Inger cleared her throat and tilted her head to one side, smirking. "The doctrine reads as follows: In the event of the throne of Cyan having no heir yet of eighteen years to rule, or the throne falling into unroyal hands, full power, rights, and responsibility are allowed to be granted to the oldest child of the king of Gallen, Cyan's only ally."

Gallen.

I stopped in my tracks, the stabbing pain in my head intensifying. I doubled over, struggling to breathe. My words came fast.

"What do you mean? Are we going to Gallen? Why have none of their royals not come to our aid by now? Will Isobel still never rule?"

Inger cackled with laughter, clapping her hands together. "Because I'm here, and the world was so shocked by the death of the Lagardes that Gallen never assumed their position. Once I recovered, I led people to believe that Cyrana had wanted me to rule. And the idea of having a *Gallenese* queen truly bothered most Cyans, so much that the discussion never left the inner circle. No one knows much about the agreement, so we can use that to our advantage."

Gallen, Gallen, Gallen. Why is that making my headache worse?

"She doesn't understand," Lady Arabella observed. "She doesn't understand why she's important."

"We can't expect her to," Norm said, gathering a fistful of my hair in his large hands. "She knows nothing of her past."

"Well we don't have to share it all," Inger said, stepping between us and grabbing my wrist. "She isn't leaving us anytime soon. Not anymore."

I wished for a fissure to open beneath me. "I thought you only needed me for experiments?"

Inger shook her head, bringing her dead eyes close to my face.

"You never understood why I picked you," she whispered, pinching my wrist. "It was not only for your knowledge in math and science, or the fact that you lost your family."

Family. The next wave of pain was so bad my vision blurred. I swayed, but Inger held onto me.

"It was not because I was lonely and thought you would be my friend," she sneered. "It was because of your medical stats, your projected height and weight. Your red hair, complexion, and freckles."

Family. Once, I had a family.

"And because you are one-hundred percent Gallenese."

***

Pizzette

"Pizzette? Pizzette Colfer?"

"That's her, right? Not some random person that snuck in?"

"Miss Colfer, can you follow the light? My flashlight, I mean."

"Open your eyes."

"Find my hand."

"Just wake up."

My subconscious mind was invaded by several voices, loud sirens, and wailing. Someone was upset.

"I'm awake," I muttered, opening one eye at a time. "Where's…Isobel?" I stared into the faces of half a dozen paramedics. "And Luck, Mattie, and Tomas?" I sat up in a chair in what I guessed was the Radio Tower's lobby, not sure how I ended up there. The last thing I remembered was passing out on the ground. My arm ached something terrible. "Are they alright?"

"Give her some water, and put pressure on that arm," one of the paramedics ordered, standing up. "And then bring her outside for bandages. We have normalcy to maintain."

Normalcy? Is any of what happened in the past hour worth so little acknowledgment?

"You never answered my questions," I called out as they walked away.

Someone handed me a paper cup filled with ice. I held it with my numb fingers and let water dribble into my mouth while they led me out to an ambulance. The back doors were open with a metal ramp laid out. Luck was sitting on the wet floor, her arms and face bandaged, eyes downcast.

"They took her," she said without looking at me. "Mattie. I thought they had you too for a minute."

I sat next to her, watching search teams combing the woods for the rest of Inger's group. They already hauled Miss Jessica over to a police car and let her sit there swearing at anyone who passed. Miss Daniels was still carrying on, crying as two medics carried Mr. Daniels away on a stretcher to an ambulance.

"Where's Isobel?" I asked, sucking on a piece of ice.

"Already home," Luck laughed coldly, twirling a rain-darkened lock of hair in front of her face. "Tomas and the reporter we talked to went with her."

"Tomas? I don't remember seeing him." I had no memory of what happened after I passed out with Isobel screaming in my ear, so close to danger and unable to help her. It irked me that I had been weak in the moment when it mattered the most.

"He carried you inside once I knocked Inger out," Luck explained. "We camped inside the lobby while Isobel and Tomas explained everything. We were afraid of Norm and Inger breaking in, so we locked the doors and blocked them with chairs. Called the police. But they never attacked us. Instead, they disappeared, and now Mattie is lost with them."

"Wow." I crushed the ice between my teeth, the chill bringing me back to reality. "I can't believe I'm alive. I fainted. I left Isobel on her own."

"She survived anyway," Luck said gruffly. "And now she's off being a princess or whatever. Cleo Pelletier, a servant who used to be one of the governesses at the palace, is tending to her now. It's all over the news."

"I bet the whole country is celebrating. Their coveted princess has returned home."

"There are skeptics," Luck murmured, biting her nails, and staring at something in the distance. "People who think an eight-year-old is not the appropriate choice for leading a country."

"What does it matter? It's a miracle she's even alive." I sighed, finishing the ice and setting the cup next to my feet. "Are people really so concerned with her age? She'll grow."

"You're supposed to be eighteen to rule in Cyan," Luck said. "They're already looking into the old library of documents, trying to find a loophole so Isobel won't face public backlash. The people of Cyan want her, Pizzette, but they know that she isn't the same as her parents and may never be. Inger knew more about politics and the economy than her, and although she was a terrible person, she got the job done."

"But Inger got away, and Norm and Arabella kidnapped Mattie." I refused to believe Mattie would have willingly gone with them.

She had made it clear she resented Inger in our little time together, and I knew she was not easily coerced.

"We sort of failed," Luck whispered, covering her face with her hand. She sniffled, her frail frame trembling. "I just want my mama."

"Me too," I said quietly, thinking of Mom who had brought me back here. My father, who saved Isobel all those years ago and died in the fire Inger started.

The mystery person who saved me in the palace hallway and warned me not to keep investigating Inger and Isobel. Now I knew why.

This city was dishonest. Once I was sucked in, it was impossible to resist the idea of being a hero. Now that I had helped return their princess, nothing had changed. I was still what I had always been; lost, scared, and not sure of where I fit in. Indebted to strangers I had no chance of seeing again.

"Sorry, love, but you should not be here."

I understood it all now.

Places like Cyan did not change overnight. It was naïve of me to think my meddling with their system would change anything. Isobel was back, and it did not matter who found her. The next round of games had already started, and Inger Kaleon still had the upper hand.

I buried my face in my knees, holding my diamond in my frigid hands.

Diamond, can you take me home?

***

Luck

When it was all over, I went home.

This ride with the driver was different. I still did not speak to the driver, but there was less tension this time. A police officer sat to my right, her sole purpose apparently being to make sure I did not hurt myself along the way. Trapped inside a moving vehicle was not exactly a harmful environment, but apparently *Princess* Isobel had insisted that police accompany Pizzette and I to our respective homes.

The large mansion was gray in the morning light, the grass overwatered and muddy. I walked up to the front door with the officer by my side. She knocked for me, understanding my silence was not hostile but anxious. I had always been an anxious person, but I had not felt this out of control in years. I needed my room, a place of comfort, and to be left alone.

Papa opened the door and immediately swept me into his arms, crying softly as he held me. He must have heard some fragmented version of the story and stayed up all night, desperately trying to reach the palace and Etiquette. He had to have seen us on television by now, and my bandaged face was not welcoming anymore. I had been through hell, and he had no way of helping me through it.

He whispered his thanks to the officer and closed the door, carrying me to my room. We passed Mama, who hesitated at the base of the stairs. She looked the same as always, elegant and calm, but her eyes were pink like she had been crying.

"Lucky, I'm so sorry I made you go," Papa whispered as he set me on my bed. He held my face in his hands, anguish marring his features. "You're hurt. We almost lost you again."

Fire. I told you, that place would ruin me. Turn everything into flames. The fire had spread to my eyes now. Wherever I looked I saw danger, figures waiting to choke me. Remembering anything about Etiquette and the awful trip cut my breathing to a minimum.

Papa pulled off my wet shoes and socks and opened my wardrobe, seeking a dry set of clothes. "The cooks are making all of your favorites, and the servants are fixing the fireplace. You're going to be okay, Lucky. This is all in the past now."

But it was not. I could still feel dreadful arms holding me back, feel the deepening surge of fear whenever someone tried to reassure me.

"I need to be alone, Papa," I whispered, pulling my feet up on my bed. "I'll be downstairs soon."

He turned around quickly, shaking his head. "Lucienne, it's too soon."

"Please." My voice cracked. "I want to be by myself."

He could see there was no stopping me. Papa closed his eyes for a moment and sighed. He still handed me several dresses and stockings to try on, then kissed my forehead.

"I love you, Luck. Don't be afraid to talk to me."

I nodded, waiting for him to leave before I dashed to the bathroom that linked my room with Maude's. I pulled open the door, the thought of a warm bath inviting.

My sister was not even supposed to be home, so when I walked in on her kneeling on the floor and crying, my heart stopped.

"Maude?"

Her head snapped up, eyes widening. "Luck? You're back?" She hugged her arms around herself, whatever she was hiding falling to the floor.

I was by her side in a second, reaching for the item before I even knew what it was.

"WAIT!" Maude screamed, intercepting my hand.

I froze, disbelief flooding me like a hurricane. "Maude, what is this?"

"Close the door." Maude smoothed back her hair, sniffing. "Then sit down and be quiet."

I listened, and returned to her, the pregnancy test stick on the floor between us.

"Care to explain?" I muttered, reading the instructions on the package. *One line means negative, two lines mean positive.*

It was positive.

"Don't tell Papa," Maude hissed. "I was checking again to make sure, but Mama knows. Not him. He'll kill me."

"You're seventeen, Maude! What were you thinking?" I stared into her brown eyes, trying to imagine my older sister as anything but the perfect, obedient daughter. She had graduated early and gone to Principles, scoring so well she was allowed to study in Gallen for a few weeks. How did she end up pregnant in the middle of the worst month of my life, and why hadn't she told me sooner?

"Well, everyone in this family is a slave to pleasure," Maude whispered hoarsely. "I guess it finally caught up with me."

I paced around the bathroom for a few minutes then sat on the closed toilet lid, frowning. "We're pretty and rich and flawed, right? I don't care about your boyfriend. I care about what kind of life you've been living while I was gone."

"It wasn't like that, Luck. I didn't run away to escape the stress of the city and sleep around with foreign men," Maude said quietly. "I...I wish I'd never gone to Gallen."

I bit my lip, running a hand through my drenched hair. "Can you tell me what happened?"

"You wouldn't understand. You're too young."

I glared at her. "No, I am not. What is there left that I haven't already seen? Our parents are getting a divorce. The crazy leader of this country tried to kill me twice. And now my teenage sister is hiding the fact that she is pregnant from our father."

Maude's eyes were hollow caverns. "So much more, Lucky. You have seen nothing yet."

"Clearly not as much as you."

"What happened was no drunken accident or product of intoxication," Maude said in a level voice. "I was taken with someone in Gallen, and we...rushed things. Had our fun because we thought we were invincible."

"You of all people should have understood the consequences. You and Mama lectured me all the time about wanting to go to a co-ed school when I was younger. You said I would be too impulsive but look at you. Perfect Maude Maybelle Legrand got knocked up before me."

"Hush. We'll talk about this later." Maude wiped her eyes, burying the test under a mound of paper towels She washed her hands, avoiding her reflection.

"Does the...father know?"

She was silent.

"*Maude.*"

"We didn't exchange links or anything. We...it's complicated." Maude splashed some water on her face, shivering. "So damn complicated."

Though I was cross with her and mad about everything, I got up and hugged her, my wet hair leaving a stain on her dress.

"Your secret is safe with me," I said softly. "I promise. I won't tell Papa."

"Thank you," she whispered, her voice thin. "Thank you, Lucky."

One month changed everything. My family, once so complete and, in my eyes, perfect, was breaking apart. The country's former royal dynasty had just been revived; the criminal who tried to destroy it lost.

If nothing else would be the same, I at least still had my sister.

"Girls!" Mama called from downstairs, her voice echoing around us. "Come down. We have things we need to discuss."

Maude inhaled sharply, a new round of tremors starting again.

"It's okay," I said, looping my arm through hers. "I'm coming with you."

***

Isobel sat on the floor of an enormous golden room, dressed in a gaudy white gown with gold lace and piping, her hair brushed and braided down her back. Everything was gold and new, from her shoes to the ribbons tying the ends of her braids to the heavy crown atop her head.

Cleo said that this was her life now. In a few minutes, they would have to go speak to the press.

Verify that the evidence sent to the Radio Tower was accurate.

Someone named Dr. Cadmire was supposed to help with that.

It was all hers; the country, palace, and Lagarde fortune. Even the dresses and jewels saved from the fire and stored away in vaults. Her full, regal name bounced around in her head. *Her Royal Highness Princess Isobel Garnet Lagarde of Cyan and the Surrounding Areas; Princess of Europia. Daughter of Prince Indio Hayes Lagarde and Princess Cyrana Kaleon.*

They offered her a meal but she turned it down. A team of servants had been overly eager to show her boxes full of treasured jewels to fit her status, but Isobel refused it all while pulling on the pearly bracelet around her wrist. Finally, Cleo selected the smallest and simplest bracelet they had; a golden bangle accented with rubies that was her mother's.

Isobel wore it next to Marmi's bracelet, rubbing them against the inside of her arm. Two mothers she would never fully remember the same way again.

"Princess," Cleo said from the doorway, ever-patient. "It's time."

Isobel rose to her feet, twisting the bracelets against her glowing skin.

Inger, her *aunt*, was out there somewhere, but the guards promised they would protect their princess. Isobel knew Inger would always be a threat until she was captured.

For now, she was warm, dressed, and in a way, not alone. Soon she would be able to talk to Luck again, and Pizzette. Find Mattie and thank her as well.

Feet padded on the carpet behind her. Isobel turned around, not expecting to see Tomas instead of Cleo. He dropped all the formalities instantly, putting a hand on her shoulder.

"Clint's back to normal," he said. "And the Service is going to interrogate those who were arrested. Don't panic now. You're safe here."

Isobel nodded, and then took his hand, walking beside him into the hallway. Cleo joined them, running through a few pointers and reminding Isobel to smile and be courteous to the cameras. Together, they reached the end of the hallway, stopping before the doors to the princess's balcony.

"Go and take a look," Cleo said with a smile. "It's all yours."

Isobel threw open the doors and stepped out onto the balcony. The wintry air greeted her, a chilly reminder of how nothing in her life would ever be the same. Isobel hesitated, wondering if she could go back to being the girl of many names for a little while longer.

I'll miss it all, but I guess this isn't the end or anything. Just the beginning.

Then she peered over the rails at the city that was now her own.

***

The End

Of Book One

Made in the USA
Monee, IL
02 October 2020